light *fell*

light fell

EVAN FALLENBERG

SOHO

Portions of this novel appeared in ZEEK: A JOURNAL OF THOUGHT
AND CULTURE (www.zeek.net) in 2007.

Published by
Soho Press, Inc.
853 Broadway
New York, New York 10003

Library of Congress Cataloging-in-Publication Data

Fallenberg, Evan.
Light fell / Evan Fallenberg.
p. cm.
ISBN-13: 978-1-56947-467-9
ISBN-10: 1-56947-467-2
1. Family—Fiction. 2. Tel Aviv (Israel)—Fiction. I. Title.

PS3606.A43L54 2008
813'.6—dc22
2006051248

10 9 8 7 6 5 4 3 2 1

For Micha and Hagai

ACKNOWLEDGMENTS

Writing a novel is a long and lonely business. I have been helped along the way by many wonderful people and institutions:

Rabbi Steven Greenberg and Lieutenant-Colonel (Res.) Hezki Malachi enabled me to enter the heads of several characters initally inaccessible to me.

Professor Norman Roth's fascinating article, "Deal gently with the young man: Love of Boys in Medieval Hebrew Poetry of Spain" (*Speculum* 57, 1), introduced me to several astonishing poems penned by famed rabbis.

Abby Frucht, Mary Grimm, Ellen Lesser, A.J. Verdelle, Phyllis Barber, Miriam Beilin Wrobel, Joan Leegant, and Eve Horowitz read the manuscript at various stages and made comments that caused me to reassess and revise. Joan and Eve were also tremendously generous in sharing their experiences and accrued wisdom.

Deborah Harris and Ines Austern provided excellent advice and comic relief, each at the right time.

Dena, Rosalie, Marc, and Esther Fallenberg did what families do: criticized, comforted, cheered.

Vermont College, The MacDowell Colony and Soho Press opened the way to opportunity.

Publisher Laura Hruska welcomed me to Soho Press and editor Katie Herman polished my manuscript with professionalism and grace.

Finally, the love, strength and encouragement I received from Yonina Weinreb Fallenberg and Yariv Levin set me on a new path of freedom and creativity.

—Evan Fallenberg

promise

promise

FRIDAY, MARCH 1, 1996

THE BOYS SEEM NOT to notice the stench of rotting fish or the shards of bottles, driftwood, and jagged shells jutting up out of the sand. In search of something along the water's edge, they remain oblivious to the icy wind that stings and bites them. Joseph, without his first-aid kit, winces at the thought of needle-sharp fish bones piercing the soft soles of their feet. But he is preoccupied with the twins, still babies, and lets the older three slip from his sight to disappear past the rotting pier. They would not hear his shouts over the ceaseless roar of the sea, so he does not bother. But should he scoop up a twin under each arm and run toward the pier? And why is he alone with all five boys on a cold winter beach? Panic foams upward inside him like bubbles on an angry sea.

He catches sight of them running away in a line—Daniel, the eldest at seven, in the lead, with Ethan and Noam close behind, their pace synchronized like miniature soldiers on a mission. Suddenly a solid wall of gray water rises as if from the heart of the sea. The boys stop their playing and turn to call for Joseph's help. But they are too far away and he cannot hear their screams. He can only see the terror that magnifies and distorts their tiny faces. He lets go of the twins as he stands to watch the wave claim his three older sons. Before looking down he already knows the babies have vanished, too, his own body submerged to the neck.

Joseph Licht awakens, drenched. It takes him a long moment to realize he is sweating under the heavy comforter and longer still to understand that his head is wet from the rain blowing slantwise in sheets through the open window. He pushes aside the comforter and sits up quickly, indignant. The carpet is soggy and the papers on his nightstand translucent. Joseph bounds out of the bed and skids in a puddle, slamming the window shut. He turns to face the priceless Géricault nude he moved from the living room only last night and sees that the rain has darkened the wall beneath it and spattered the gilt frame but has not reached the canvas itself. Hands on pajamaed hips, he stares hard at the painting through lowered lashes. An art treasure, in his bedroom, nearly destroyed. He imagines restorers in white lab coats working to return it to its original glory and Pepe, shocked at last, throwing him out into the street. Sitting on the edge of the bed, he gathers the reassuring comforter around him and takes stock: the painting is unscathed, the papers will dry just fine in the sauna, and if Joseph can let himself believe it, on this very Sabbath, right here in his beachfront apartment high above Tel Aviv, he will be celebrating his fiftieth birthday with his five sons—all old enough to be fathers themselves—marking the first time in nearly two decades that they will all be together with their father.

Joseph's image in the bathroom mirror this morning does not entirely displease him. Though no longer a man who turns heads, he knows he looks good for someone his age. On a good day he can pass for ten years younger—thirty-eight even. Joseph has found the right shade for his hair, a metallic color suggesting gold and silver and reminiscent of the blond he once was. This keeps him from looking like an old fop, the kind whose very forehead takes on a hennaed sheen. The wrinkles in his face are still fine lines. He is no longer thin, but neither has he gone soft and doughy.

In the kitchen Joseph perches on a stool at the counter, upon which he has arranged computer printouts of his to-do list and the weekend menu. He pours hot brewed tea into an antique porcelain teacup, tracing the floral border with his finger. The rising steam paints a cloud on the window and Joseph looks beyond it to the dull gray sea, the empty beach bereft of little boys on crucial missions. Down the coast even Old Jaffa is mellow and subdued on this midweek winter morning, crazy strung colored lights breaking up and refracting back at Joseph through drops on the windowpane. With a red marker he crosses off completed items from his list: cookies, potato kugel, ratatouille.

He has given long and careful consideration to planning the menu for this reunion, each item chosen for the effect it will have on his guests' emotions as much as on their palates. Twenty years ago he left his wife, Rebecca; their five sons; his father, Manfred; the moshav where he grew up; all his friends and acquaintances—in short, his life of thirty years—when he fell in love with the Rabbi Yoel Rosenzweig, a dynamic young teacher-scholar hailed by all as an *illui*, a Torah genius, perhaps the greatest of his generation. In his old life Joseph had never held a dinner party, never hosted other than on the sporadic Sabbath. Back then the objective of hosting was to create an environment entirely recognizable to all the participants: no vegetables other than squash and carrots for the standard chicken soup, no exceptional sauces for the required chicken, no exotic seasonings for the potatoes. The only surprise in the Friday night meal came at its conclusion, after the singing of the traditional Shabbat melodies, when the sated guests had been mollified. Only then might they be expected to face with equanimity a chocolate cake or poppy roll or apple pie.

Joseph's rebellion was thorough: he has neither eaten nor served those foods on a Friday night since. Now the most humble of his meals is a lemon and artichoke chicken that he is careful to serve with Thai rice or Chinese noodles, or fresh corn on the cob in summer. A meal hosted by Joseph may begin with a sorbet or fruit salad, the main dish accompanied by honey-glazed sweet potatoes or fresh greens with a drizzle of orange and mint. His desserts are the talk of his circle, designed to leave his panting guests cursing themselves for poor pacing.

Joseph lifts his teacup in a toast to his own cleverness. He has, after all, succeeded in planning a perfectly traditional set of Sabbath meals while maintaining his own hard-earned panache. And most important, every dish will be on the table for a precise and celebratory reason, either because it was a food one of the boys once loved or because it will jiggle loose a crystallized memory or because it will provide a topic of conversation if none is forthcoming. There will be chicken soup and chicken, but the soup will be a highly refined version of Rebecca's—the noodles, rice vermicelli, and the chicken, stuffed breasts. Potatoes, too, but in the form of *roesti*, which Joseph learned to prepare from Rebecca's mother and ultimately personalized by adding onions fried lightly in beer. Knowing that his middle son, Noam, loves red meat, he will grill cubes of the choicest beef seasoned with basil and coriander. Through effective detective work he has learned that Gavriel is still a chocolate fanatic, so in his honor Joseph has included a dark chocolate mousse with amaretto. And for Gavriel's twin brother, Gideon, who has abandoned the family tradition of modern Orthodoxy for ultra-Orthodoxy—and as far as Joseph is concerned, aesthetics and good taste for stringent religious observance—he is inaugurating newly purchased sets of cookery, cutlery, and crockery, dutifully immersed in a ritual bath precisely according to Jewish law.

There will be a lot of other dishes, too: a light Corsican ratatouille, fennel salad, tossed greens with heaps of olives and croutons (the boys used to pick these out and fight over them), three vegetable casseroles in the unlikely event that Gideon's wife—Joseph's sole daughter-in-law—doesn't eat meat, and a wonderful Brazilian fish recipe that includes mustard, wine, peanuts, and coconut. The last is a dare: he will mention Pepe and Brazil only if things are going exceedingly well. Last night he baked oatmeal cookies for munching and one of today's projects is a huge iced angel food cake, the kind the boys always requested for their birthdays. This time the Birthday Cake, as they called it, is for Joseph himself.

He slides off the stool, removes the glazed-glass bowl of

blueberries from the refrigerator, and rinses them carefully at the sink. After all his cautious planning, these unanticipated fruits are the most special food of all, a good omen for the coming reunion. They are at once a beloved treat, a memory, and a topic of conversation. A fluke. A sign. Just as Joseph was roaming the *shuk*, filling his basket with edible memories, he saw them, ". . . big as the end of your thumb / Real sky-blue, and heavy, and ready to drum / In the cavernous pail of the first one to come!" It was that poem that had spurred him, at the height of his infatuation with Robert Frost, to take the family berry picking in western Massachusetts in the frenzied days before Rebecca and the boys returned to Israel, leaving Joseph alone in Cambridge to finish his doctoral dissertation. The oldest boys, Daniel and Ethan, had wanted to see ". . . fruit mixed with water in layers of leaves, / Like two kinds of jewels, a vision for thieves," and Rebecca had readily agreed, eager to blot out the tantrums and rages to which Joseph had been subjecting them all and hoping the boys could take back with them to Israel new and better memories of their father: Joseph at peace in nature rather than seething with frustration in front of the old Hermes typewriter they had filched from Rebecca's mother, or raising his hand as if to strike them.

The berries ripened outrageously early that year. Even Joseph had known that the fruit should not have matured until August, so he wasted no time in arranging the outing when his adviser reported, after an early July weekend visit to his summer house, that the surrounding countryside was bursting and ready for picking.

A photograph from that day stands out among all the others on a glass-topped table in Joseph's living room. It was snapped by a local farmer's son awed by the sight of the young couple with their five boys, slight variations of one another, all blond, all healthy, all full of confidence, energy, and curiosity. Rebecca had laughed when the young man said she and Joseph looked like brother and sister, but this had annoyed Joseph; he had always been uncomfortable admitting they were second cousins, a fact of which their resemblance was an unwelcome reminder. Now, after more than twenty years, he can see how he and his wife were similar and how they were not; much like a peacock and his peahen, their features were nearly identical, but on him sharper, clearer, more highly colored. His hair lighter, his eyes brighter, his smile broader, his teeth whiter. She was a faded version, a smudged copy. Still, the photo features youthful parents, not yet thirty, smothered by the chubby twins, at twenty months already trying to keep pace with the older ones, hugging, squeezing, and toppling one another. Daniel at seven, Ethan just turned five, Noam not quite four. All seven Lichts in full laughing motion, limbs flailing, eyes crinkled in absolute gaiety. No movie camera could have portrayed the excitement or hidden the anxieties with more fidelity than did the still camera of that Massachusetts farm boy on that summer day in 1975.

Just yesterday Joseph watched his Nigerian house cleaner, Emanuel, pick up that photograph from the glass-topped table, watched him dust and study it. Emanuel dusted others, too: the boys collecting eggs from the henhouse as toddlers; slightly older, riding bicycles, tractors, horses; and later still, somber faced in army fatigues, as if ready for anything in the name of God and country. He dusted the single black-and-white photograph of Pepe's daughter, Carolina. But Emanuel did not pick up and look into those other photographs as he dusted them, only the one of the berry pickers, the model family with its promise of perfect happiness.

love

love

1976 — 1977

THE FIRST TIME JOSEPH heard of the Rabbi Yoel Rosenzweig was in the Talmud study group after Sabbath morning synagogue services on his first Saturday back in Israel, when he was still adjusting to the strangeness of return after three years pursuing a doctorate at Harvard. He marveled at his boys, who, in the few months since they had returned early with Rebecca, had come to seem as though they had never lived anywhere else, never spoken another language. He wondered if they had had time to establish rituals of their own, whether they had found some of the secrets of moshav boyhood or whether those secrets die with each person's own youth.

One thing was clear and constant to Joseph above all else on that Saturday morning. He could not imagine being anywhere but the Sabbath morning Talmud study group, still led by Rabbi Crystal after nearly thirty years. Even the study room smelled the way he remembered it—the odor of books left to mold in their musty bindings—and Joseph was not at all surprised to find the three-legged chair Rabbi Crystal used for his books propped up under a window, where it had always stood. Joseph himself had broken the fourth leg while decorating the synagogue for Independence Day nearly twenty years earlier, in 1957. What Joseph could not understand was that if nothing at home had changed, then why was it he had to ask people to repeat themselves, did not catch the hidden meanings in their words, had trouble interpreting their exchanged glances? There was a foreignness in their speech and manners, and Joseph was beginning to wonder who had changed after all. Had Sde Hirsch, his moshav, been metamorphosing in his absence, or was it he? Would he fit in here again?

He was sitting in his old seat, pondering the wisdom of their return to the moshav, when Zev Frankel, who always made the blessing over the wine after Sabbath services, mentioned Rabbi Yoel Rosenzweig. "That boy's an *illui*," he said. Frankel had been Joseph's Bible teacher for four years in elementary school, and in Joseph's memory the only other human being ever to have earned the title "Torah genius" from Frankel was the great Maimonides himself. "Rabbi Rosenzweig isn't even forty years old yet but I'm willing to believe he'll be the head of the Rabbinical Court or chief rabbi in a few years." Frankel added with awe, "He knows the five books of Moses by heart."

"Aw, that's nothing." For fifty years Mordechai Kapinsky had been looking for ways to outdo Zev Frankel, ever since he had lost the battle for Fanny's heart to Zev's superior education. "I know a dozen guys who can chant the whole five books without a sour note." He grinned at Zev and Joseph noticed he only had a few teeth left in his mouth, and those were dark and twisted like the blueberry brambles Joseph had grown to love in New England.

"But this Rosenzweig, he's read every volume of the Talmud a few times and I hear he's writing a commentary of his own, like he's back in the fourteenth century or something," Zev countered. "And he can quote just about everything that's ever been written about Jewish law. I went to one of his lessons once, his Wednesday evening lecture at the Yeshurun Synagogue in Jerusalem. He was talking about the laws of betrothal and brought in Jewish sources and goyish ones, too—Shakespeare and Milton and some French writers I never even heard of, without a single book in front of him." He waved one thick finger in the air. "Now that's what I call an *illui!*"

Joseph lost no time in arranging to be in Jerusalem for Rabbi Rosenzweig's lecture the following Wednesday. He hoped to have a moment to speak with this young rabbi, barely older than he, at the end of the lesson, to ask for some help in finding suitable texts for the book he was working on. He was having trouble with classical sources and historical background material, and he was sure someone who had such knowledge at his fingertips could be helpful. And, of course, he was curious.

Noam and the twins insisted on riding in the back of the station wagon when Rebecca brought Joseph to the bus stop. Joseph grew irritable and impatient as the boys fought over territory, certain he would miss his bus. But once on the way he relaxed and enjoyed the bus ride to Jerusalem, his first trip to the capital since his return to Israel and his first extended period of time out from under the roof of their small moshav home crammed full with five boisterous boys. The weather had turned cool and a surprise rain shower the day before had summoned some greenery from under the cracked brown earth. Little buds and sprouts gathered into soft carpets that escorted the road past Tel Aviv, past the meteorological station, near the monastery at Latrun, and up to the foothills of Jerusalem, where the road began to ascend. There the forests were thick on either side of the road, green and welcoming, but the abandoned armored tanks strewn among the trees were reminders of a more treacherous era, a period of menace and havoc. Joseph thought about the Yom Kippur War, which he had sat out in Cambridge, then caught himself and decided to prepare the questions he would ask Rabbi Rosenzweig.

The bus arrived at Jerusalem Central twenty minutes late, but the lesson would not begin for an hour, so Joseph was in no rush. He walked down Jaffa Street to the shouts of the vendors at the farmers' market, stopping to marvel at the brightly colored produce, fresh and ripe and beckoning. In America he had been in awe of the availability of everything all year round—strawberries in winter, avocado in summer, bananas on your cereal twelve months a year—but he had felt cut off from the seasons and feared his children would grow accustomed to the abundance, would not appreciate the taste of the first sun-ripened orange in December, after swooning from the fragrant blossoms for weeks. He plunged in to the market's inner alleys, dark and sodden and filled with the smells of fish on ice, coriander, parsley, and mint. Offended by the noise, he passed by several stalls before stopping at the stand of one quiet apple vendor, eager for the crunchy sweetness of a Mount Hermon apple. Joseph selected two pale red apples, each stippled with green, as his mother had taught him that these were the juiciest. He really only wanted one apple but felt obliged to buy an extra, since the market was a place where one bought in quantity. The apple vendor glared at Joseph from beneath one bushy eyebrow that arced the width of his forehead like a parasol and said, as he took Joseph's money, "Congratulations. Maybe next time you'll let your wife do the shopping."

Joseph put one of the apples in his coat pocket and bit into the other as he made his way to the stop for the not-so-frequent #14 bus, which would bring him to the gates of the synagogue. *Blessed are you, o lord our God, king of the universe, who created the fruit of the tree.* And, since this was his first Mount Hermon apple of the season, his first in perhaps four seasons, Joseph added: *Blessed are you, o lord our God, king of the universe, who has kept us in life, sustained us, and brought us to this season.* Outside the market, on the bus that took him through the center of town to the Yeshurun Synagogue, Joseph began to notice how much Jerusalem had grown in his absence. The city seemed to have sprouted traffic lights everywhere, though Joseph could have sworn that only a few years had passed since Jerusalemites had walked to the intersection of King George and Jaffa streets every Saturday to watch the colors change from green to orange to red on the city's only traffic light. Outside the synagogue Joseph was surprised to find a line of people waiting to get in, and he cursed himself for having wasted his time in the market when he could have been there all along. By the time he managed to enter the cavernous main hall there were no seats left at all, only space for standing, and that barely. The upper gallery, where the women sat, was full, too. Joseph found a small alcove near the front of the stage, off to the side, and took refuge.

There was an excited hush in the great hall. Joseph noticed that most of the men wore crocheted *kipas* like his own, though there were plenty of ultra-Orthodox men in black hats, as well as secular Jews in shiny satin or velvet skullcaps that would disappear from their heads on the doorstep of the synagogue. He tried to imagine this much interest in a lesson at the university and remembered being offended by a joke that an ultra-Orthodox man in Boston had told at his expense upon learning that Joseph was studying at Harvard: "This great rebbe was on a plane with a Harvard professor"—Joseph recalled the man's sneer at the academic title, how he had stood too close—"and when the prof complained that things weren't like they were in the fifties, when the students gave respect to their teachers, the rebbe told him: 'That's your fault for teaching them about evolution. My students see me as one generation closer to the revelation at Mount Sinai, one rung higher on the ladder of holiness. Yours see you as one link closer to the apes.'" At the punch line the man had poked Joseph so hard he had had to rub the spot.

Joseph overheard the conversation of two young men standing near him. Their jeans and bright-colored shirts gave them away as university students, despite their large skullcaps and the ritual fringes hanging out over their trousers in the style of the ultra-Orthodox.

"I've been following Rav Yoel around since his first Wednesday night lessons in a bomb shelter, just after the Six-Day War," said the taller of the two. "He's moved four or five times since then. They always need a bigger place for the crowds. There's almost nowhere left in Jerusalem for him to grow."

"Maybe the municipality should put up a building for him!" replied the other.

Joseph spent the remaining time before the lesson thinking about his book, what was missing, what he had left to do. He felt confident about his thesis, that the religiosity of the romantics had informed their poetry, that the rhythm and meter of the language of the Bible had a parallel in their work. He knew the sections on Blake, Wordsworth, and Shelley to be solid, well researched, and adroitly written. He envisioned the prophets Ezekiel and Isaiah visited by these Englishmen, imagined their stilted conversation. How the Englishmen would have been startled to learn that they understood the biblical prophets not at all! Joseph had met well-meaning Christian Bible scholars overseas whose eagerness and earnestness could not bridge the chasm between the jagged, dusty ancient Middle East and the soft curves and polished shine of twentieth-century America or Europe. The romantic poets would be the same, their self-confidence betrayed by the rough manners and abrupt speech of the prophets. But Joseph was worried about the section on Hebraism and Hellenism, which he had intended to appear right at the beginning of the book but had avoided writing until this last possible moment, so great was his dread at the prospect of straying from his field of expertise. Still, to discuss the rebellion of the romantics against the neoclassicists, he knew he would have to touch on ancient Greece. It was on this point that he wished to solicit Rabbi Yoel's aid.

At two minutes before the hour, complete silence fell

over the vast crowd. By this time all the standing room in the great hall was used up, and people were jammed together, buoyed by one another. Most had notebooks, and Joseph spotted a row of yeshiva boys lined up one behind the other, each preparing to use his friend's back as a desk.

The rabbi entered through a door at the back of the stage, empty handed. Joseph was quite near him, eye level with the rabbi's knees. He could see that Yoel Rosenzweig was a surprisingly large man who looked more suited to a life of physical, outdoor labor than to the scholarly and spiritual pursuits that undoubtedly required endless hours of sedentary study. Joseph was accustomed to rabbis whose bodies resembled the punctuation marks at the ends of the questions they were constantly being asked or asking themselves; this rabbi's shoulders, in contrast, held him straight and tall, his chest broad and solid, his legs thick and sturdy as the young eucalyptus trees in the garden outside the house at Sde Hirsch. Still, he was terribly pale, his skin nearly translucent, his chapped lips a dull dusty rose color. He wore a closely trimmed beard that was mostly the color of coffee with milk but speckled with either blond or gray, Joseph could not tell. He did not wear glasses, and when he stepped to the microphone he did not acknowledge his devoted audience in any way. He merely plunged into his lesson, as though he were sitting in a yeshiva study hall with a group of five or six students.

The rabbi's voice sounded groggy and reticent to Joseph, but he was captivated by its low-simmering peacefulness, like a rich, dark, mysterious brew. He found it very difficult to focus on the meanings of the words descending on him in a mellifluous flow. He noticed Rabbi Yoel's long fingers—

thick, but not coarse like those of the farmers at Sde Hirsch—as they gripped the sides of the lectern or punctured the air to make a point. For the most part, the rabbi stood still, but at times he swayed to the rhythms of the verses he quoted, and Joseph found himself closing his eyes at those moments, to allow the holy words to penetrate him. He found new meanings there, in phrases he had known since childhood; they pierced and prodded and even consoled him like they had never done before. When the rabbi finished, a short ninety minutes later, Joseph was surprised to find he had drifted into a state of partial consciousness, swaying on his feet and transported.

The silence that followed the rabbi's concluding words lasted only a few seconds. Immediately there was a rush of excitement, and all around him Joseph saw small discussion groups forming. The audience was not interested in stepping outside the doors of the synagogue back into the everyday world; these people wished to prolong this uplifting experience, and Joseph understood them. Despite his own feeling of awe, he still wanted to seek a word with the rabbi and began to make his way through the throng that now separated him from the stage.

He waited patiently as dozens of men jostled for the chance to ask a question. Then he noticed that the small crowd in front of him was not dissipating, that most of the men were just waiting to hear whatever the great rabbi had to say to anyone about anything. Joseph pushed ahead, eventually reaching the small inner circle of devotees. From there he could see Rav Yoel's eyes. The sadness in them stopped Joseph short and he found himself searching them out, hoping the rabbi would look directly at him.

He got his wish, but the result was a shock, something he would never forget. The moment their eyes met, Joseph could feel them lock together. His vision blurred, and all he could see were these two eyes, cannonballs hurtling through the murkiness of his mind. It was the first time Joseph knew for a fact that he had a soul, because these eyes had reached it, surrounding and assessing it. He at once sensed his own soul's shape and depth and density. He could hear nothing but the roar of the cannonballs, and his legs seemed to grow roots below the marble floor. At the same time, Joseph could sense movement within his body, the flow of blood through his veins. He felt like an hourglass, filled with quickly sifting sands, and imagined his life in the measured time that was dripping always downward. He knew in a flash that this moment in his life was the narrowest strait of the hourglass, the point to which all the sands had been flowing from the time he was born, the point from which they would continue to be shaped until there was not a single grain left to pass through.

Joseph blinked and recovered himself slowly. "I am truly grateful for the lesson," he said in a voice just loud enough for the rabbi to hear. He was still puzzling at what he had felt a moment before, hoping to reconnect with that soul whose existence he no longer doubted. "It was my first time." The rabbi nodded a thank-you and acknowledgment, as if he knew Joseph had never been in his audience before. "I am nearly finished writing a book, *Poet and Prophet*, and I have a few questions. Perhaps I could impose . . ."

Just then a short, burly man pushed his way through to the rabbi and grabbed his arm. "You'll be late for the radio, Rabbi. Radio doesn't wait."

The rabbi nodded to the man, then turned to Joseph. "Please come by later this evening, at around eleven o'clock. The address is on this card." He pulled a small rectangle of thick paper from his pocket, pressed it into Joseph's palm, and fell in line behind the burly man without another word. The groups of people left in the synagogue parted to let them pass and they hurried out the door. Joseph noticed the other men in the inner circle staring at him, quiet and brooding. They looked like jilted lovers, and suddenly Joseph realized the value of the invitation in his hand. He made his way to the dark street and at the first streetlight stopped to inspect the card. He gasped at what he saw: above the embossed address, in very small print, were his own initials, JL.

In the crevice of time between his first meeting with Rabbi Yoel in a crowd of one thousand fans—secular, traditional, Orthodox, male and female, young and old, all come to lick, savor, and swallow every honeyed word the young Torah genius had to offer—and the promise of a more intimate acquaintance later that night in the rabbi's own home, Joseph decided to pass the time in Independence Park, where he could enjoy the sandwich Rebecca had packed for him and the second apple bought earlier that day at the farmers' market.

Jerusalem that evening, like most evenings in the sleepy capital, was quiet. Joseph saw few cars and no pedestrians in the streets, so he was surprised to bump into four or five men milling around the paths of the park itself. The park was darker than he had hoped, the only lamp a bulb at the entrance to a shabby public restroom, and the meandering presence of these ghostly souls gave Joseph an inexplicable feeling of malaise. He decided to cut through the park to

the opposite side, toward an exit that would lead him into
the bright lights of the city center. He followed one unkempt
lane after another, scraped several times by long branches
that grew like accusing fingers into his path. Nervous, he
quickened his pace, dashing around blind curves. He blun-
dered into the neglected Muslim cemetery at the edge of the
park, tripping over a trampled section of fence he mistook for
a tree root. Here, with taller trees and thick foliage, there was
even less light. In his increasing panic, Joseph caught his foot
on what felt like a step and fell flat, sprawled across the tumbled, nameless grave of some long-forgotten sheikh.

For a second Joseph lay still, the wind knocked out of
him. Before he felt the hands, he smelled the cigarette. "You
don't know your way around here," said a low voice above
the arms that were snaking around him, lifting him from
underneath. At first Joseph could only hear the voice and feel
the hands, and he wondered for a second if this were the
sheikh himself, angry at being roused so artlessly. After all,
this was Jerusalem, an ancient city with ancient secrets and
countless spirits.

The hands, it turned out, extended from a flesh-and-
blood human being, who, it seemed, was a bit shorter than
Joseph but nearly twice his girth. As Joseph lay facedown,
winded, the man bent down between Joseph's parted legs,
sliding one arm well below his belly while hoisting him up
with the other in one quick motion. Joseph found himself
standing straight, his back pressed up against the stranger,
the man's arms still folded around him. The smell of tobacco
was stronger now, and Joseph thought he could feel the
wisps of a mustache on his neck. He was afraid to move.

"Once you come here for the second time you won't

trip and fall anymore," said the man, moving a hand down
Joseph's body. Until the hand stopped at his groin, Joseph
thought he was being robbed. All at once he understood, and
a violent shudder shook him from head to toe. He thought
about the lesson he had just attended, given by a genius of
Torah unparalleled in his generation. What a sacrilege it
was that the men in this park were determined to bring upon
themselves the wrath of God within the shadow of the
Yeshurun Synagogue, disobeying his law within earshot of
hearing it. How this people never changed—the same Jews
who witnessed the miracle of the exodus and the parting of
the Red Sea only to wail about the marrows and melons they
had left behind as slaves in Egypt. Emboldened by the young
rabbi who seemed to have all the answers, Joseph broke
away from the hands and the body, running back through
the breach in the fence along the paths once again, passing
curious idlers who flashed him knowing glances as he hurried by. He reached the street exit at the far side of the park
breathless and trembling.

All at once a memory accosted him, unbidden, from his
years at Harvard. A late afternoon in his first winter there,
just as he was becoming accustomed to the tension and
terror that would characterize his Cambridge years. *Is my
English good enough? Am I clever enough? Do I really understand
what this lecturer/administrator/colleague/cafeteria worker is saying?* And at home, with five boys under the age of seven: *Why
is this place always such a mess? Why are the kids so noisy? Quiet!
I've got to have some quiet to read this article/write this paper/con-
sider this issue.* He had just emerged from a dizzying meeting
with a professor of Bible studies recommended by his own
adviser, in a part of the campus to which he had never before

ventured. A Christian, he thought throughout the meeting. A Christian who knows so much about *our* Bible, but who does not live it the way we do. Joseph the scholar could not erase his many years of yeshiva study, and this professor's expertise, *authorship* of the Bible—as if anyone but God could have penned the Holy Torah!—shocked him.

For the last twenty minutes of the meeting it had been clear to Joseph from the churnings and rumblings of his stomach that he would need to find a bathroom quickly. He had had a weak stomach ever since coming to Harvard and had limited his diet to only the simplest and healthiest foods, but to no avail. Worse, he had drunk several cups of coffee that day and knew he would soon pay the price.

After a hasty goodbye he had bolted to the end of the hall and down a flight of stairs in the unfamiliar building, darting from side to side of the second-story corridor until crashing through the door of the men's room. Darkness had bloomed early and no one had yet turned on the lights in the restroom. He was pleased to find it unoccupied, so that he was free to relieve himself without inhibition. Joseph reveled in the calm and quiet as he allowed his body to reach an equilibrium of sorts. Here in the toilet stall he was free to think. Snippets of the divinity professor's words came back to him and he was no longer appalled, just pensive.

Suddenly the bathroom door creaked open and a man walked to the urinals straight ahead of Joseph's stall. Joseph leaned sideways toward the space between his stall door and the door frame—instinctively, he would think later. Between two large hinges, the narrow space allowed only a knee-to-chest view in profile, the sole identifying feature a large brass belt buckle. The bathroom door swung open again. It was a large bathroom with a dozen urinals, so it puzzled Joseph that the new man, in dark trousers and a plaid shirt, would select a spot so close to the brass buckle.

From his perch on the edge of the toilet seat, Joseph then witnessed a coupling of the sort he had never thought of, never dared imagine. Dope smokers, male and female students living together, divinity professors discussing authorship of the Bible; all these had jarred him since he had arrived at Harvard, but the gyrations of these two men—two men!—in a public restroom were too much for Joseph. He could see their erections, the groping hands of these two strangers in a lavatory, and this made him fear the end of days, for God would certainly have seen too much of our species to allow us to continue polluting his world much longer. Sodom and Gomorrah revisited, the curse of Leviticus, God's unremitting fury unleashed upon humankind.

When the two men moved to the stall next to Joseph's he was afraid to shift on the seat, afraid to breathe. They were noisy, these daring lovemakers, each pant and groan a small stab at Joseph's propriety. More than anything he was offended by the deep pleasure implied in their throaty grunts, like those of contented animals. When they threw their weight against the partition between their stall and Joseph's, he feared they would crash through and taint him with their perversion.

They climaxed nearly simultaneously, one in a high-pitched whine and the other in a series of gasps and spurts that Joseph at first mistook for a heart attack. He never heard either utter a single word, from their initial encounter at the urinals through the tearing off of wads of toilet paper and the final zipping up. One darted out quickly but the other remained in the stall, deathly quiet. Joseph wondered how long he would have to balance there at the edge of the toilet seat, motionless, until his neighbor finally left. His exposed rear was cold and numb, his neck stiff, and he was expected home for supper. Finally, after several minutes, the man opened the door to his stall, emerged, and headed toward the hallway. But as he passed Joseph's stall he pounded once, very hard, on the door, causing Joseph's heart to leap: "Enjoy that?" the stranger asked in a low, sarcastic growl.

He had tried to calm himself before calling home from an outdoor pay phone. "Tell Mother everything is fine," he said to Daniel. "I am running late, no time for a meal now." Rebecca was busy cleaning up after bath time while the boys took turns pulling the phone from one another, testing the novelty of hearing their father's voice far down the line. It was that hour when they needed a last whoop for the day, when the splash of bathwater and the sweet scents of soap and shampoo gave them a late burst of energy, and they ran from room to room, tallest to smallest or smallest to tallest, shouting and laughing and pushing and tripping in a wild frenzy, until one fell or slammed into a piece of furniture or stubbed a toe. He and Rebecca had long since given up trying to shepherd the boys to bed or even calm them down when they were like this, and it was at these times they felt the enormity of the world they had created.

When Joseph put the phone down he tried to breathe deeply, aware of the open space in the darkened center of the campus that spread out around him. For once he found himself missing the boys' outrageous antics, the same ones that on other days provoked him to raving outbursts.

He was still shaky as he neared his office. He needed

time alone to digest what he had just experienced. His dazed reflection greeted him from a window in the stairwell, all but the space around his eyes, where two deep hollows appeared, as though someone had taken scissors and cut blackened oval holes in his face. He wondered if he could continue working in this hell. Rebecca would be ready to move back to Israel tomorrow if he would only give her the word.

When he was safe and alone behind a bolted door, Joseph had sat at his office desk in a stupor, head in hands. Again he considered returning his family to the moshav—he could finish at Tel Aviv University or perhaps in Haifa—but even as he forced up scenes from his disturbing afternoon, he already knew this was an option he would not take. This was Harvard; this was America. He was building a brilliant future for himself exactly where he wanted to be. Besides, he reasoned, this behavior must be universal; there were probably also restrooms at Israeli universities where men met to mate. No, he would stay in Cambridge.

Calmer now, relaxed, Joseph had let his mind drift. He leaned back in his chair and closed his eyes. He pictured the men, their blunt erections like exclamation points in a silent dialogue. He saw their pelvises tilt toward one another, their eager fingers grabbing, massaging, exploring. And then, through his fear and disgust and confusion, he became aware of what had been there all along: the tingle and swell of arousal, the first inklings of an instinct as basic as theirs, and as complex.

Still shaken by the incident in the park and the memory it provoked, and out of breath from fear and anticipation, Joseph arrived ten minutes before eleven o'clock at Elharizi

Street, too early to knock on Rabbi Yoel's door. He sat on a bench at the corner, checking his watch every minute or so until, at three minutes before the hour, he could allow himself to find the house.

Elharizi Street was one of the most elegant addresses in Jerusalem, really a shaded country lane of fine stone mansions in the heart of the capital. Still, Joseph was amazed at the enormity of the building in front of him, and fished the card out of his pocket to make sure that he was indeed at the right address. It was a three-story home with a large garden, several balconies, and a tall, sloping roof, in contrast to the flat-topped buildings on either side. Joseph stood at the gate, contemplating ringing the buzzer, when the front door of the house opened. "Come on, come on," said the rabbi in a loud whisper, motioning for Joseph to lift the latch and come through. Joseph was glad at once and smiled to himself as he gently pushed the gate and replaced the latch carefully behind him. "I'm so pleased you came," said the rabbi when Joseph reached the door. He leaned his face close to the other man's, grasping Joseph's shoulders and pulling him across the threshold. Joseph sought out Rabbi Yoel's eyes, but the strange pull he had felt earlier that evening was gone.

The rabbi led him down a long corridor, past several large rooms. Joseph saw a grand dining room with a tremendously long carved-wood table and high-backed chairs, a glass breakfront stuffed with silver standing nearby. He had the feeling he had left Israel and was in a European capital of ballrooms and royalty. Some of the people in Sde Hirsch had managed to bring over pieces of furniture from the German towns or Polish shtetls they had left before the war, but none of this elegance and grandeur. He recalled a saying in the

Talmud: "A lovely wife, a lovely house, lovely accessories, these broaden a man's heart and encourage wisdom." Joseph was wondering whether the rabbi's wife was a real beauty when the rabbi seemed to read his mind.

"My wife's father is a wealthy and generous man," he said as they entered the room at the end of the corridor. "Belgium. Diamonds. My wife and children are there now in fact," he added quietly. "It was his dream to marry his four daughters to rabbis and support them all forever. Luxuriously. I stopped feeling guilty about it several years ago, because I have to admit I am glad not to be occupied with financial matters. I devote myself entirely to learning and teaching." He motioned Joseph to a large comfortable chair in a corner of the room. "I'll be back with refreshments in a moment."

Instead of sitting, Joseph inspected the room. It was a study, with high ceilings and Persian carpets and an antique desk polished to a bright gleam. But most notable were the bookshelves lining all four walls, full to bursting from floor to ceiling with books of every color and size. From what he could gather, more than one whole wall was taken up by biblical commentary, and commentary upon the commentary, two thousand years of biblical exegesis that made Joseph's limbs feel heavy. He ran his fingertips over the gold lettering and leather bindings but did not remove a single tome from its place. On the next wall he found several shelves of Passover Haggadahs. He pulled out one oversized volume, an illuminated manuscript with instructions for leading the Seder night in Italian. The third wall seemed to be organized by subject, but here the logic and order of the other two shelves broke down. There were a few series, but mostly there were individual titles. Here he found physics and history and linguistics and astronomy but more than anything else literature and literary criticism, in English, French, Latin, German.

A small volume sitting on the desk caught Joseph's eye. It was tiny, nearly compact enough to fit into the palm of his hand, and the cloth cover reminded him of thick wallpaper he had seen once in a European castle. It was a book of French verse dated 1629. He understood nothing of the poetry, but was interested in the frantic scrawl in the margins, a bewildering combination of French and Hebrew written in varying shades of ink that had left smudges, stains, and even punctures in the paper.

"You've discovered my passion." The rabbi, so tall he had to duck coming through the doorway, was carrying a silver tray that held a china tea set, fresh sliced cake, and a bowl of fruit. "I am in love with books. And that one's a personal favorite. It was written by a monk who had taken a vow of silence. The man was tortured by his private thoughts. He spent his life seeking refuge from his mind and his soul." He placed the heavy tray on a table in front of the chair Joseph was meant to occupy, then straightened to his full height. "He went in for floggings and periods of starvation and had several 'insignificant' appendages removed from his body, the better to feel pain and distraction. His one pleasure in life was the writing of these poems, which he did at night, a poem a night in place of sleep. It's easy to see him as crazy today, but I respect his single-mindedness, the way he tried in earnest to control his passions, the love and sensuality he was so determined to squelch. There are few men of his stature today."

The rabbi lowered himself gently onto the sofa. Joseph

marveled at the grace of such a large man. Rabbi Yoel poured tea for them both and added sugar to their cups. Joseph replaced the small book on the desk and sat in the chair opposite his new friend.

"Were those your notes in the margins?" asked Joseph.

The rabbi raised his eyes slowly to meet Joseph's. "Some. Some," he admitted reluctantly. "The others I assume belong to the person whose name is inscribed on the first page, a village priest who lived in Aquitaine in the mid-eighteen hundreds. I did a little snooping around about him once and found out he'd been committed to an insane asylum, where he died by his own hand." The rabbi cut a wedge from a small tart apple and offered it to Joseph. "He was definitely coming unhinged when he owned this book. He makes comments like 'delicious,' 'naughty,' and 'angelic,' then toward the end of the book he begins filling up the margins, page after page, with verse of his own, in the same spirit as the monk's, but vile and vulgar. He uses the foulest language of the period; I've had it verified. And on a blank page at the very end of the book he wrote a confession of sorts that makes the Marquis de Sade seem tame. The man knew his Scriptures and was determined to desecrate everything written there."

The two men spoke for hours. Joseph privately rejoiced at this new and rare friendship with a man in whose company he could feel completely at ease and yet challenged intellectually, free to speak Hebrew or English or both in one sentence and free to speak his mind about the rigors and joys of Orthodox Judaism in the same breath as the glories of Western culture. Free to admit that a houseful of small children was daunting and free to hint that being a husband was not quite the joyful experience he had hoped for. Each of Rabbi Yoel's questions nudged him toward truths lying dormant in his soul, while his own queries slowly unknotted the rabbi's reluctant tongue.

After they had drained a second pot of tea, the rabbi fetched two crystal shot glasses and a bottle of schnapps. He filled both glasses to the rim. "Here's to true friendship," he said, then whispered the appropriate prayer and downed the contents of his glass.

Joseph did likewise, then leveled his gaze at the rabbi. "And what exactly," he said, his eyes watering from the schnapps, "*is* true friendship to you?"

Rabbi Yoel—large, gentle, troubled—frowned. "First let me tell you what it is not. It is not students who wish to gnaw at your brains, not colleagues who talk sweetly but shoot malicious glances at you. It is not sycophants who worship you or doubters who wish to trip you up. It is not even one's children, not one's wife, not one's siblings. It is not schoolmates gathered across long years of poring over texts together."

Joseph's brain felt as though it were bobbing on a stormy sea. Each time it surfaced, some new face appeared: a bearded rabbi, a small boy with sidelocks, a wigged woman. He fought hard to quell the effects of the alcohol and pay attention.

"True friendship," Rabbi Yoel continued, almost oblivious to Joseph, "should be a near-perfect pairing. Of minds and interests. Of caring and willingness to do for the other. A physical ease, too." He seemed to notice Joseph again and assessed him. "I haven't experienced the beauty of true friendship. Have you, Joseph?"

Joseph closed his eyes for a moment. His brain was no

longer bobbing and the images had disappeared. It was only Rabbi Yoel's face he saw now, kind and handsome and inquisitive, and when he opened his eyes the man's expression matched what he saw in his mind's eye and was awaiting an answer.

"Never," he said.

Neither man spoke for several moments. Rabbi Yoel filled their glasses. He smiled broadly. "So, friend, why don't you tell me about that book you're writing?"

Joseph and Rabbi Yoel discussed *Poet and Prophet* in great detail and the rabbi was only too happy to offer suggestions. And then the rabbi told Joseph about his latest project, a study of the Talmudic expression *nafal nehora*.

"It's Aramaic, literally means 'light fell' or 'light was sown.' It's used in several strange and wonderful stories in the Babylonian Talmud." He lifted his glass of schnapps, saluted Joseph with it, and downed it in one go. After inhaling deeply and refilling his glass, he continued. "In one story, Rabbi Amram the Righteous, a judge and rabbinical decision maker at the court of the Babylonian Exilarch in Nehardea, is asked to house, in his attic, some Jewish women who had fallen into the hands of gentiles and whose status had not yet been decided—whether, under certain circumstances, they should be permitted to return to their husbands after being freed from captivity. The ladderlike stairs to the attic were removed so that no man could ascend and take advantage of their precarious situation before their fate had been determined. But there was an opening that led to the attic, and when one of the women walked near it, *nafal nehora*—light fell—and Rabbi Amram could see that light from below. With the power of sudden arousal he took the stairs, which normally required ten or more men to move, lifted them up alone, and began to climb. Halfway up he spread his legs—Rashi explains in order to stand firmly where he was so as to overcome his lust—and raised his voice and shouted, 'Fire in the house of Rav Amram!' The other sages ran over to put out the fire. They said, 'You have shamed us since it is clear to all what you intended to do!' To which he responded, 'Better that you should be ashamed of Rav Amram in this world than in the world to come!' Immediately thereafter a column of fire lust burst forth from Rabbi Amram's body and left him."

"A man of true integrity," ventured Joseph.

"Mmmm, yes, he certainly chooses the difficult path."

Joseph was intrigued, and not in the least sleepy despite the late hour. He took a sip of schnapps. "Tell me another."

The rabbi cocked his head as if assessing his audience. Joseph could see he was making a decision. Once decided, he emptied another glass, moved to the edge of his chair, and spoke as much with his hands as with his mouth.

"When Rabbi Yohanan, head of the yeshiva at Tiberias about sixteen hundred years ago, went to visit his pupil Rabbi Elazar, who lay ill in bed, he saw that Rabbi Elazar's home was dark and windowless in the manner of the poor. Rabbi Yohanan raised his arm and *nafal nehora*—light fell. Rashi explains that his skin glowed and was very beautiful. And with the room thus illuminated by the light cast from the glow of his beautiful arm Rabbi Yohanan could see that Rabbi Elazar was weeping. 'Why do you weep?' he asked him. 'If it is because of the Torah—that you did not study as much as you wanted to because of life's travails—we have learned that he who studies much and he who studies little are equal in their merit, as long as both direct their hearts to heaven. And if you weep because of your humble finances, we have learned that not everyone merits two tables, one of riches and one of Torah. And if you weep because of your sons who died, this, too, is not a reason to weep.' Whereupon Rabbi Yohanan produced a bone from the tenth of his sons to die, which he carried everywhere with him."

"But of course it's none of those," said Joseph, who was intimate with Talmudic syntax.

"Naturally," Yoel responded. "Rabbi Elazar revealed the reason he wept. 'Because of that beauty'—Rabbi Yohanan's exposed arm—'that will wither in the dust when you die; that is why I weep!' And Rabbi Yohanan said, 'That is indeed worthy of weeping over!' And they both wept."

Joseph remained silent and contemplative but Yoel's face implored him to respond. "It's more than just a weakness for beauty. There's an element of power, even violence here," Joseph said.

"I'd call it sexual attraction. Lust. A fire raging within." Rabbi Yoel looked so intently into Joseph's eyes when he said this that Joseph thought he might feel that same charge he had felt after the lecture. "And I don't believe that the sages condemn the particular brand of attraction that existed between the two rabbis. They treat it as natural, a divine beauty whose eventual disappearance really is something to weep for."

"And you plan to write about that? Who will publish it?"

Yoel leaned back in his chair and laughed. "Yes, who indeed?"

"But how . . . how did you choose such a topic?"

The rabbi shifted in his chair, averted his gaze. "I did not choose it; it chose me. Beauty, attraction—my mind has been dwelling on these matters lately. A preoccupation." He paused, seeming to force himself to meet Joseph's gaze. "More like an obsession," he said firmly, but in a whisper.

"Your wife," Joseph said. "Is she beautiful?"

"No," the rabbi said evenly. "But she has a certain style."

"So—excuse me for asking—are you attracted to . . . someone else?"

The room was so silent it seemed as if all creatures every-where had stopped moving and breathing as they waited for the rabbi to respond. Yoel, however, sat motionless, dazed. Had it not been for the twitch at the corner of his mouth and his gaze—his eyes skittered from object to object in the room, stopping everywhere yet taking in nothing—Joseph would have thought the rabbi was experiencing some alternative consciousness. After several very long, wordless moments, Yoel spoke, his voice soft and full of credulity.

"It's all been in the realm of theory for me, just ideas based on reading and study, as is all my work." He stared at Joseph for a moment. Then his lips parted, a look of confu-sion creeping into his eyes.

Joseph rose abruptly from his seat, feeling that confusion penetrate him as well. "I should probably be going. It's quite late," he said. He walked down the long hallway, Rabbi Yoel close behind.

"You're right. I had no idea," the rabbi said, glancing at his watch. "Would you care to sleep here? You can see we have plenty of space."

Joseph felt unbalanced, as if suddenly he no longer knew himself. He was rarely this at ease, especially with someone he had only just met. He longed to stay in this house with his new friend but felt it would be an intrusion. And there was something else, something that made him reticent. "No, really, I must be getting back. . . ." All at once he remembered the card the rabbi had given him earlier. He fished it out of his pocket.

"I'd almost forgotten. These initials, my initials—JL— how did you manage—I mean, I didn't see you write them. In fact, you didn't even know my name then. . . ."

Rabbi Yoel took the card from Joseph. "That's not my writing. I have no idea—" He stopped midsentence, frowning, as though recalling something.

"What is it?" From the look on his face Joseph thought the rabbi was experiencing some intense pain.

"I'm no expert in Kabbalah. That is really not my field," he answered slowly. He seemed to be reading from a page long since photographed by his amazing mind. "But it seems to me that, that . . ."

"Yes?"

"It's absurd. Kabbalistic nonsense, I suppose, but it reminds me of something I read once by an obscure Kabbalist of Safed. He claimed that God has three ways of letting two people know they are divinely suited to one another: by a tune they both know but have not learned from anyone around them; by a dream they have shared on the same night; and by a written word that appears to them both and has meaning only to them."

Joseph felt light-headed as he tilted his head back, raising his eyes slowly past Yoel's throat, his bearded chin, his full lips, his pale cheeks. When he reached Yoel's eyes they seemed to be asking a question, and Joseph, as sure as he knew his name, knew he had the answer. He tilted his head back farther, closed his eyes, and moved his mouth closer to Yoel's.

The first kiss was no more than a brush of lips, so soft it

could have been the beating of butterfly wings. He did not open his eyes to see the bliss and turmoil on Yoel's face. He could only register the lips as they brushed his again, this time lingering, touching. At the third kiss Joseph leaned in just slightly, the press of Yoel's lips stronger this time. Thus they stood, their bodies touching only at the lips, and Joseph thought he could be happy to stand like this, kissing but not kissing, forever.

A thought floated across his mind like a banner: A MAN IS KISSING ME. Indeed, the sensation was like none he had ever known. Yoel's lips were full and dry, fleshy pillows for Joseph's own thin mouth, his beard and mustache soft as tickly feathers that smelled of soap and tobacco and something mysterious and exciting he could not name.

He opened his eyes just a bit to catch a glimpse of Yoel's mouth through the veil of his lashes. It was open in a half pant of desire, a small dark cave in the midst of the forest of his beard. He could see it was moist and warm beyond those thick, dry lips and Joseph longed to lose himself inside, swallowed and devoured headfirst. He rose on his toes to meet Yoel's mouth again. I AM KISSING A MAN. He pulled away for another glimpse, as if to convince himself. Yoel opened his eyes and together they stood staring at what they were about to do and where it would lead them. Open eyed, they kissed again briefly. Then, in silent agreement, they stopped. Yoel put his arms around Joseph and Joseph pressed his head against the expanse of Yoel's chest and they stood, barely breathing, adrift at the gateway to their new world, until a distant car horn brought them back to their old, real world and Joseph slipped out into the night, knowing nothing would ever be the same again.

*

Although they began to speak by telephone daily, several weeks passed before they could schedule another meeting. Both had been awed by the ardor of their encounter, the long and passionate parting embrace that was less a goodbye than a bridge to whatever would come next. They had an inkling of an idea what would happen between them, though neither could truly imagine the experience. It was too new for them.

They arranged to meet at an unoccupied apartment owned by Yoel's in-laws, in the midst of the first true winter in Israel in more than a decade. Pounding rain kneaded and sculpted the dunes up and down the coast, bridges were flooded by swollen streams, and the road to the Dead Sea remained closed for an entire week. In Jerusalem snow fell four times, twice a fine powder that vanished within hours and twice a thick and heavy quilt that snapped the branches of unaccustomed firs and pines and paralyzed the city for days.

Joseph overshot the narrow alley twice and gingerly skirted a shin-deep puddle. Blinding rain nearly obliterated the small ceramic street sign. Finally he spotted the diamond-shaped lamp that Yoel had described over a doorway and felt a flood of relief. Like a medieval guild member, he thought as he pulled the bell cord to be let in: Yoel's father-in-law advertises his profession even here, a continent away from his business interests.

Inside, Joseph's noise and bustle broke the heavy silence of the staid stone house. He shook water off himself, scattering droplets around the slate foyer floor. He stomped his feet and tossed his umbrella into a brass barrel. He barked a cheery hello to Yoel, who stood to the side, pensive, wrapped in a thick wool cardigan, hands thrust deep in his pockets. Joseph felt exhilarated by his battle with the elements; even his fingers and toes throbbed. His eyes were bright and shiny, his cheeks flushed with color and health. His head felt clear. He'd made it, he had succeeded in fighting the rain, making the necessary arrangements, and here he was, in a large house in the Old City of Jerusalem with his new, dear friend. Everything in him shouted, *Life! Optimism! Happiness!* and for once he was inclined to listen.

Even Yoel's tepid response to a strong and solid hug did not deter Joseph, who felt emboldened by the drama of the weather. He rubbed his hands together, offered a true and generous smile, and demanded the cup of tea with sugar cookies he had been promised.

"I've made a hot spiced wine. Neither of us has to drive or go anywhere on this dreadful evening. I thought it would be relaxing."

Joseph was heartened by this small surprise. Yoel looked as though he needed to loosen up and enough wine might do just that. "Perfect!" he exclaimed, again too boisterous and self-assured for the shadowy room.

The large salon was filled with furniture, knickknacks, and sculpture, but Joseph was drawn to the view of the Wailing Wall from an enormous window that framed the two-thousand-year-old ruin like a kitschy watercolor. Yoel stood near him but gazed at the wall through a different window. A dozen or so men stood praying despite the pummeling rain, and one ragged figure sat slumped in a chair in the women's section, a plastic shopping basket at her side.

Yoel spoke in a quiet voice spiked with anger. "Their supplications leave me cold. Why don't they spend more time trying to improve the world around them instead of praying to 'renew our days of old' or 'bring the Messiah now'? Such a waste of God's precious time."

Joseph turned sideways to look at his friend. Yoel continued to stare straight forward, and Joseph could see the bitter rage in his clenched jaw and narrowed lids, his hands still rammed into his trouser pockets.

"They're all lacking something, wishing for something. I can't help feeling sorry for them," Joseph said softly. He took a step closer to Yoel and looked up into his half-turned face. "Anyway, let's celebrate our good fortune with that wine you've prepared for us."

Yoel relaxed his shoulders, turned toward Joseph, and smiled in acquiescence. "You'll like this," he said as he poured from a crystal decanter. Joseph bent his head into the rich scent of cloves and citrus and cinnamon that wafted from his glass. As he tilted it to his mouth Yoel stopped him with a gentle hand and recited the appropriate blessing.

Joseph dropped onto a plush sofa, hoping his friend would join him, but Yoel seated himself in an armchair to his right. He offered Joseph sugar cookies. They spoke of the apartment, Yoel's in-laws, the weather. As they sipped the hot wine Yoel recited a poem too quickly for Joseph to catch and decipher, a poem he said had been written by a Muslim cleric for a young Christian boy. Joseph retained only the closing stanza:

> If only I were the priest, or the metropolitan
> of his church, or else his Gospel and Bible;
> Or if only I were the sacrifice he offers
> or his cup of wine, or a bubble in the wine.

Yoel pointed to a small stack of books on the coffee table in front of them, each with protruding slips of colored paper. "I've been asked to speak to a group of American Jewish leaders next week and I hoped you could help me by translating a few passages into your perfect American English."

A bit deflated at the prospect of spending this precious evening poring over heady texts, Joseph nonetheless made a quick peace with himself and said he would be delighted. Yoel moved to sit beside him on the sofa, in order to explain what he needed, and Joseph could not help but notice the way his long, thick fingers caressed the holy books, the deep resonance of his voice as he read the verses. Joseph could barely restrain his urge to lean on Yoel's shoulder, to feel the pulse of his big body.

"So that's all you really need to know. I hope it's not asking too much. You can write it all down on this pad of paper. Just please write neatly so that I'll be able to make sense of it later." He stood quickly and Joseph nearly fell into the crater of space left in his wake. "I'll leave you alone with it for a little while. I know how hard translating is, especially with someone looking over your shoulder." Yoel's mood was lighter now, almost cheerful, and he bounded out of the room at a joyful clip.

Joseph opened the top book on the pile. It was something he recognized, a passage from Maimonides about the place of man in the universe. The text was straightforward, but he could not reproduce the great scholar's tone in English. It came out sounding too common, too modern and American, and he wished he was capable of a Shakespearean translation, something to elevate the English version. The next text was Buber, so he skipped ahead, hoping that would be more

accessibly modern. Agnon, Ahad Ha'am, Flavius Josephus—
here they were, a pantheon of Jewish minds, each with
demands of his own. Joseph began each with hope and interest and ceased each translation midtext. His disappointment
with the turn of events grew with his frustration.

Half an hour passed, then another. Joseph sat with one
foot buried beneath him in the sofa cushions, the other on the
floor. The books lay open on his lap and on either side of him
and in front of him on the table. Words mounted one another
on the page, rolling and tumbling and frolicking together in a
passionate riot. He had had too much wine and felt at once too
relaxed and too agitated to be competent, so he tugged at
locks of his hair, gathering clumps, first pulling, then releas-
ing, hoping to call himself to attention. He kept his head
bowed to the page in front of him, watching the words perform stunts, enjoying the negative image as he moved his eyes
from print to blank space and back again. He did not hear
Yoel approach as much as feel him draw near. Joseph could
sense the tread of Yoel's stockinged feet as they led him
toward something altogether new.

Yoel cleared a space and sat down on the edge of the coffee table, legs wide apart, encompassing all of Joseph and the
books surrounding him in the angle of his large body. He
leaned across the narrow space of floor between them and
closed the book on Joseph's lap, and Joseph noticed, without
looking up, that Yoel had failed to bring his fingers to his
lips, despite the fact that the book he had just closed was a
holy text. He watched as the last printed words that had been
taunting him faded into the black cover, the edges of the classical Hebrew letters disappearing first, then their legs and
heads and finally their trunks. Still Joseph did not look up,

for he was afraid of what would happen. He knew the look he would find on Yoel's face and he knew he would feel responsible, guilty. A fine rabbi, a brilliant scholar, a—

He saw Yoel's hand reach out, and when it touched him, landing gently on his right cheek, Joseph was surprised it did not scorch him. The hand was cool and dry, its touch light but firm. Joseph held his breath while the hand moved across his face, skimming the surface of his skin. It slid to the back of his neck, still light and gentle, but insistent now, just a little, moving Joseph's head forward in imperceptible degrees, the fingers moving, massaging. Joseph's eyes were closed, but he smelled Yoel's beard as it grazed his cheek and he turned into it like a blind man to sound. It seemed to Joseph that there were no other movements or sounds or emotions anywhere, that at that particular point in time the universe was focused on this house, this room, these two men.

A wave of cool air rolled against Joseph's neck and cheek as Yoel leaned away from him. He brought Joseph's hands together and held them in his own, concealing them and taking possession. He kissed Joseph's fingers, curling and unfurling them, bringing them to his own face. Joseph looked with his eyes and with his hands into the visage of this man he had known such a short time, and all the desperate longing he had known fell away from him, stone walls of protection crumbling to sand and dust, and in their place rose a bright, hard passion. Joseph removed his hands and waited for Yoel to open his eyes, then kissed him, watching his eyes, kissing him at the sides of his mouth where the hairs of his mustache grew long and gold. Then he, too, leaned back, and waited.

Yoel took Joseph by the shoulders and eased him down

into the sofa until he lay flat, then dropped to the floor, only his head above the cushions. He spread his arms like the wings of a soaring eagle and touched Joseph's head and feet. He lay his head on Joseph's stomach and played his hands up and down his body, stopping to explore and examine. Joseph felt Yoel was learning him, that he was committing the text of Joseph's body to memory. A genius, an *illui*, so why not this, too? Why not use his gift on Joseph? Yoel's large head lay comfortably upon him, like a precious egg, Joseph's middle section a nest, and Joseph was reluctantly reminded of Rebecca, how her body seemed always to jab him so that he was forced to change positions every minute or so.

Yoel raised his head and for a moment looked at the body laid out before him. He seemed to be at a crossroads. He lost no time, however, in choosing a direction and began undressing Joseph—methodically, slowly, just as he might undress his own children. First the socks, then the sweater, the trousers, the shirt, folding each article of clothing and putting it on the table behind him without ever taking his eyes from Joseph. He paused briefly when he reached the *tallit katan* and seemed poised to kiss the fringes of this holy ritual undergarment. Joseph knew he was contemplating the daily admonition not to stray after one's heart. He could see behind the wise, saddened eyes the centuries of rabbinical commentaries and moral tales and *midrashim* and *aggadot* about that passage that must have been rushing through the genius rabbi's brain, and certainly many others about the evil inclination. But Yoel banished these thoughts; Joseph could feel the weight of centuries of learning and tradition being rolled heavily to the side. Yoel removed the fringed garment resolutely, but more carefully than all the others, and placed it atop the pile. All this he did without any help from Joseph, shifting him slightly from side to side, arcing and bending his limbs. Soon Joseph lay bare chested and bare legged on the sofa, one thin layer of cloth still covering the intersection of his legs and trunk.

Yoel stood up, and to Joseph he seemed taller and more massive than ever. He believed that if Yoel were to spread his hands in the air, above Joseph's body, Joseph would levitate to his palms like iron to a magnet. Yoel gazed down at Joseph, and as he undressed himself he said, "For all the knowledge I have amassed, I do not understand the Holy One, blessed be he. I have asked him one hundred if not one thousand times since I met you what he had in mind in bringing us together." Yoel looked to the window, forming his arms into a gesture of supplication. "If this is a test, if bringing me together with the other half of my very soul in the form of a man is your way of making me prove my love and devotion to you, by denying my love for him, then I would say you have chosen the hardest test of them all, the one I was bound to fail from the beginning. But if "—and Yoel stopped to look at Joseph—"if you mean to show me that this is my true path, that you have brought us together to love one another, why did you make me a teacher? Why give me the ability to understand your words with such clarity and to help others know you, too? Why did you give us wives and families?"

Joseph thought that God was there, looking at Yoel at eye level. He wanted to cover himself, but just then Yoel removed the last stitch of clothing from his own body and stood naked, towering above him. Joseph looked him over, everywhere but his face, the one part of Yoel he knew at all. He felt Yoel's body was familiar, though, just as he had imagined, and so Joseph relaxed. Yoel bent down and lifted Joseph from the sofa then carried him to a soft rug and stood him there, kneeling in front of him. He removed the last of Joseph's clothing and Joseph looked to the clock on the mantelpiece, as if to record this moment in his own personal history.

Yoel sat back on his heels, gazing at Joseph, then pulled him close and began kissing him, first as he had before, then with increasing vigor. His touch was no longer light, but openly insistent, desirous. He hugged Joseph around the waist and eased him down, kissing everywhere his lips reached. He lay back and drew Joseph with him, then rolled over on top of him. They pressed themselves to one another as if to bind themselves together for security against all the dangers of the world, or perhaps as protection from an angry, jealous, and vengeful God. But mostly they delighted in their bodies freely and wholly, each surprised at the insistence of his own, each pleased with the passion of the other's. At one point Joseph thought he felt tectonic plates clicking into place beneath him and the alignment of the stars and planets above him, as if the whole universe were falling into its rightful place just as he and Yoel were finding theirs. They fell asleep together enmeshed, and woke together that way, too.

"What were you doing that whole time I was translating? It seemed like hours that you left me there."

Yoel released his grip on Joseph, rolled onto his back, and said to the ceiling, "I was praying in a tiny room at the top of the house, begging God for some guidance, some wisdom. Strength to fight this. I recited psalms and medieval *piyutim* and the confessional portion of the Yom Kippur service and a few incantations I learned from a sixth-century kabbalistic text. I strung together whatever seemed relevant." He took a deep, steadying breath. "And after I don't know how long I asked myself what I wanted to happen, what I really wanted. And from the noisy jumble in my head the answer came as clear as the blast of a ram's horn: Joseph. I want your beauty. I want your mind. I want your friendship." He paused, quieter now. "I have never thought this about another human being, but I want your body and I want your soul. I crave you."

He pulled Joseph in close, and Joseph nuzzled into the soft fur of his chest. "I don't know whether this was showing appreciation for a most marvelous and wondrous creation of God's or the opposite, idol worship," Yoel whispered languorously into his ear, filling him with fresh desire, "but I felt words of prayer and thanks on my lips the whole night. Blessings and songs of praise for the beauty God has created in his world. Yehuda HaLevi must have composed this one, nearly nine hundred years ago, with you in mind: 'With all the delights of the world I will ransom / The night when my lust was fulfilled / By the gazelle of loveliness, and I scraped / From his lips the flowing wine of his vineyard / And kissed his ruddy cheeks.'"

Joseph rolled to his side and wrapped Yoel's arms around himself. "And I was thinking that I never live in the present—mostly in the future and occasionally in the past, but never in the present. But last night I was nowhere but here, the whole night, completely and totally with you."

Yoel murmured agreement, but Joseph felt his body stiffen. "And now it's the day after and we will dress and go to our endeavors and the doubts will creep in, and the guilt. And the guilt will last until the next time we meet, when we have begun to wonder, begun to know, in our separate prisons, that we have crossed a dangerous boundary into a country that demands too much of citizens like us—shame and abhorrence followed by complete repentance, or the shattering of our lives as we know them." He said this with such matter-of-factness that Joseph at first thought he was joking. "Time will tell if the power of our love and attraction is enough to sustain us in place of our relationships with God."

"Why 'in place of'?" asked Joseph weakly, fearing the answer and the whole discussion. "Can't we love one another *and* God?"

Yoel propped himself up on one elbow and looked into Joseph's face. "No, my friend. The question is not whether we can love him, but whether he can love us, and if the humans he has created in his own image can love us. And the answer is a clear no on both accounts. Now let's shower and dress and eat breakfast and start trying to continue living our old lives with our new knowledge." He stood up and offered a hand to Joseph, embracing him as he rose to his feet.

"We must always be there for one another, no matter how awful it gets," he said, and Joseph, deciding not to wonder how awful that might be, planted his feet resolutely in the present.

Joseph and Yoel continued to communicate and meet as often as possible, usually at the apartment of Yoel's in-laws. In particular, there were four Friday mornings, maybe five, when they worked together to decipher several marvelously sensuous poems penned by the great rabbis of medieval Spain. On the last of those Fridays, as they walked together to the apartment, Yoel took each long, shallow stair leading down through the *shuk* at Jaffa Gate in one extended stride, while Joseph broke them up into a left-right rhythm. He wished to stroll there with Yoel, to absorb all the sensations, but they were rushed for time, with less than three hours for studying, chatting, lovemaking, eating, showering. He wished they could pore over the handiwork of the hammered-gold tea trays, carved olive-wood boxes, and tiled backgammon sets. He especially wished they could explore the spice shops, their pungent aromas spilling out into the covered alleys and mingling with the mint leaves of the shopkeepers' tea and the donkey droppings that dotted the cobblestone walkways. Had he known how little time was left to them he would have dashed through the *shuk*, ignoring all sights and sounds and smells. He would barely have contained himself until they had locked the front door behind them and he could press himself into Yoel's flesh in an attempt to make them one.

All of their meetings included certain rituals, beginning with Joseph's offering: fresh pita bread and sour cream or mint leaves from Rebecca's garden or a page of questions from his research jotted in haste then recopied in a legible hand. Yoel brought appetite and answers. They would sit facing one another, close but not touching, to catch up on day-to-day matters: news, their children and wives, health, books. Then, as if on cue, they would come together for lovemaking, sometimes slow and careful, other times in a passionate frenzy.

On that last Friday, Joseph presented Yoel with his most special possession: a small, imperfect antique jug of aquamarine glass salvaged from the sea and pocketed by his childhood friend Arik, who had given it to Joseph to thank him for endless hours spent helping him pass his matriculation exams.

"It's about fifteen hundred years old, probably from Qastra."

The jug was dwarfed by Yoel's massive hands. Holding it from the bottom, he carried it to a window and opened a shutter to catch the light. A band of shells and chips of colored glass girding the center of the jug shone like a jeweled halo. Yoel was silent for a moment, then turned toward Joseph and recited, in a choked whisper, the blessing over objects of beauty: *"Blessed are you, o lord our God, king of the universe, who has such in his universe. It is beautiful beyond words, Joseph, but you are more so."*

Joseph stood riveted. He did not wish to move from this time or place. He thought he might cry or shout or ascend to heaven from sheer happiness. Instead he went to the window, rested his head on Yoel's shoulder, and gazed with him at their treasure.

It was also on that Friday, the last of those unforgettable Fridays, their final meeting, that they did, in fact, for the first time become one. Joseph felt as if the chasm at the very center of his being had been filled with Yoel's love, and he rejoiced in his newfound wholeness and contentment.

So deeply satisfied was he with their newly enriched relationship that it suddenly became clear to him that it was now time to leave home and start anew, and so absorbed was he in this realization that he failed to taste the bitter drops of anguish on his lover's lips.

The next evening, after nightfall had converted the holy Sabbath into an ordinary weekday, Joseph—still riding the wave of wholeness and contentment he had caught with Yoel on Friday morning—left his home and family and settled into a new life in the first flat he found, two bare white-washed Tel Aviv rooms with a sofa bed, a collapsible table, one chair, a radio, a small and noisy refrigerator, and a single gas burner. In the days that followed, as Joseph slid from nervous hopefulness to quiet panic, he experienced a churning dread in his stomach that he preferred to attribute to approaching meetings with lawyers and an accountant, meetings that would annoy him with their pursuit of bothersome details and the embarrassment of intimate questions. Worse still, Joseph had been unable to make contact with Yoel since he had left Rebecca and the boys, left home.

On the third morning of his new life, Joseph was cutting slices from a loaf of bread when the seven o'clock news began. He was pouring boiling water from a kettle over powdered coffee and a half teaspoon of sugar during the first item, about a foiled terrorist attack in central Jerusalem, and by the third he was reaching, bent at the waist over the tiny refrigerator, for an open carton of milk. *Popular Jerusalem rabbi Yoel Rosenzweig was found dead in a pool of blood and glass in an apartment in the Old City before dawn this morning. No details are being released but police have opened a full-scale investigation. Rabbi Rosenzweig, thirty-five, was born and educated in the capital. His lectures, writings, and televised weekly Torah portion lesson drew a very large following. The day and hour of the funeral will be announced upon completion of the police investigation.*

The carton landed upright with only a splash of milk beside it. Joseph landed upright, too, on his knees, his legs suddenly unable to support him. The radio announcer droned on, the refrigerator hummed and clanked as before, but Joseph heard a heavy door of thick metal slam shut somewhere. After a while—a few minutes? an hour? —he crawled across the floor to his sofa bed, dragged himself up onto it, and stayed there, curled on his side, for most of the day.

In the first terrible days that followed it was all he could do to make himself continue living. He had no appetite but he took tiny bites of dry crackers with cottage cheese. He had no desire to breathe fresh air or see other human beings but he made himself take a walk around his new city block each evening at dusk. His whole being had gone numb, his voice fell into disuse, and he was surprised to find himself whole and healthy each morning as the sun screamed through his curtainless windows.

Three days later, on a Friday morning, Joseph's father came to find him. It was hot and dry that day, the sun lolling in a bed of burning haze. Joseph did not rise from his bed at the sound of knocking, but he had not locked the door in days and his father entered on his own. Joseph had not changed clothes or shaved or washed since hearing the news of Yoel's death, and he rolled toward the wall at the arrival of this dreaded visitor.

Manfred stood in the middle of the room saying nothing at first, his full attention on his only son's spartan apartment. He moved to the window, which overlooked a parking lot, and spoke from there, as if in time with a metronome. "Well, I see you've done quite well for yourself here. But it's time to come home, while we'll still have you."

In the days that seemed like months since he had come to Tel Aviv, decimated by loneliness and fear, terrified by a choice gone wrong, strangled by the silence and unmeasured time that were now his, Joseph's fevered mind had again and again carried him back to Sde Hirsch. He knew he could rouse himself from this bed, step out into the land of sun and shade and people and life, and board a bus for his moshav. He knew his wife would accept him back without words, bruised but not broken. His father would greet him without comment. His boys would whoop and gather around him, all eager to be the first hugged. He could resume his life, sleep in his bed again, stroll in the citrus groves of his youth, smell the scent of fresh hanging laundry as it snapped in the sea breeze from the west. He could look forward to pomegranates ripening into full blush under pointed crowns, their blood-red seeds eager to spill into the impending new year. It was all there for him to choose, a life waiting for his selection like a closet of clothes to be worn one day at a time until his death.

And only then, for the first time, did Joseph know he would not return to that life, even without Yoel.

"Leave, Father," he said to the wall.

"I am certain I did not hear you properly," Manfred answered, his German diction slicing the Hebrew words into sharp, neat cubes.

Joseph sat up in a mangle of sheets and faced his father. His hair was slick and matted, his mouth coated and foul smelling. His shirt twisted sideways, the third button sacrificed to the bedclothes. Anger raged from his every pore, and Joseph spoke with a clear and controlled menace through gritted teeth. "I said leave my home. Go back to your moshav and do not bother me here again." He stared into his father's face through wide-open eyes and neither blinked nor swallowed.

Manfred opened his mouth to speak, then closed it. His bearded jaw quivered and Joseph detected a tic flickering lightly under his left eye. But his father said nothing. Instead he turned his back and left the flat, closing the door as lightly as if he were parting from a sleeping infant.

"No!" Joseph yelled. "That's not how you do it!" He

bounded out of bed, threw open the door, and shouted into the empty hall, "I'll show you." And he slammed the door shut, again and again and again, until the hinges rattled, and the doorknob came loose, and the ringing in his ears matched the shouts and moans and sobs that wrenched themselves free from his throat.

Joseph experienced the weather as an internal phenomenon that spring as he stumbled from home to work and back each day. He mistook the raging heat for the aftermath of an explosion he had detonated in the middle of his life, felt it shrink and shrivel the lobes of his brain until there was nothing left in his head but a few dried peas and a lot of swirling hot dust. He woke up parched each morning with a pain in his throat that felt like a fish bone caught sideways. His eyes stung and his nose bled often. Joseph's sense of loss was so great that sometimes he would pinch himself in the leg or arm, surprised to find all his organs and appendages intact.

Between the *hamsins* there were days of great beauty and clarity that spring. Crocuses blossomed along the banks of the Yarkon River in festive quantities and a fresh sea breeze blew gently across Tel Aviv, fanning away the smog and the grime, but Joseph was oblivious to the change. There is nothing redeeming about me, he thought as he plucked blackened bread from his ancient toaster. I deserve this punishment, he told himself in an office at the university, when a shelf of books loosened itself from the wall and tumbled onto his head. The pain was a welcome relief, a diversion.

He had been hired as an associate professor at Tel Aviv University and was assigned to teach two introductory literature courses and an upper-level tutorial on the English romantics that semester. He had prepared his lectures in the preceding months, had sounded out ideas on Yoel. Now he was walking through them in a daze. He found he could suffer the time in front of the class if he just concentrated on reading his notes. He was aware of the need to clear his throat often, as though a layer of fine sand and dust had settled there. Attendance flagged as his voice flattened to a monotone, his range as thin as parchment.

Joseph declined all invitations. The department head requested his company for a home-cooked meal; colleagues offered coffee, a movie, even a weekend in the Galilee. His only social engagements consisted of meetings with lawyers, his and hers. He agreed to everything, all conditions. When Rebecca's lawyer insisted that Joseph be forbidden from meeting with more than three of his sons at a time, his own lawyer tried to rally him to protest, but the Rabbinical Court had stipulated no visitation rights until the divorce was settled so Joseph consented and consented. By the time her lawyer was pushing a clause that would bar the boys from ever sleeping over at Joseph's home, neither he nor his lawyer reacted at all.

During that spring only one thing surprised Joseph, the realization rousing him from his stupor: that it was not only Yoel he mourned, but his boys, too. Living with them, he had been an impatient, short-fuse father, offended by their noise and too preoccupied to respond to their constant pleas for attention. "Daddy, watch this!" they would cry as they turned somersaults or flew paper airplanes or jumped from hills of dirt. "Over here, Daddy, look!" they would call as they carried trays of eggs from the chicken coop or shimmied up the trunks of towering eucalyptus trees. He would glance, smile, and return to what he was doing, even if he was not really *doing* anything. In fact, during his last months at home, he was always thinking, planning. When would he get to see Yoel next? What elaborate web of lies would he have to construct to arrange an overnight tryst? What clever gift could he bring to his lover at their next rendezvous?

But now that he had lost them, his boys became his obsession. He longed for their endless questions, ached to watch them curled in their beds, kicking off sheets and blankets almost as fast as he and Rebecca could cover them. He was desperate for dawn, the silence of night's end pierced by their croaking voices. "I'm the first awake *again*!" Ethan would call brightly each morning. "Quiet!" Daniel would mumble, and the twins would spring awake, rattling the bars of their cribs with a song from nursery school. He pressed his hands flat to his face as he thought of bath time, when the old claw-foot bathtub became a sailing ship, a submarine, a sea. Their whoops and shouts resounded in his brain, bouncing madly in that empty cavern. He recalled the last bath, Noam and the twins screeching their own version of the chant they had heard Daniel and Ethan create when it was their turn in the water: "Don't want shampoo, don't want soap. Don't want nothing, nope, nope, nope!"

Up until the Saturday night he had left home, he had counted on love, had not, in fact, given it a thought. His wife had loved him quietly. Yoel had loved him with passion and fanfare, with bells and whistles and fireworks, and, also, with the dark, sad beauty of a requiem. The boys had loved him, though they would never have known to name it love. Joseph knew that even his father loved him without ever once in his life having told him so. And he, Joseph, had loved them all in return, in different measures and shapes.

So now that he had stuffed all this unwieldy love into a large cloth sack and tied it closed, now that he had choked off this protean but constant supply, he began to ponder the nature of love. He wondered if he could survive without it, wondered if their stifled love would wither and die or whether it would swirl around, puffing up and out and eventually spilling back into his life. He wondered if the different loves he felt for them—and surely, he thought, the love he felt for Yoel and the love he felt for the boys should have different names, their natures were so vastly different—would grow or diminish, would fossilize or metamorphose.

The divorce came to court during the second week in May. A headache the size of a fist had wedged itself behind Joseph's left eye, and he felt himself involuntarily winking at the three rabbis on the dais in front of him. Rebecca seemed plumper but pale, and she wore a suit he knew she hated, a hand-me-down *pieds-de-poule* from a Swiss aunt. Her hair was freshly washed and gleaming. She was hatless, though Joseph was certain her lawyer would have instructed her to cover her head in respect for the court just as Joseph's lawyer had instructed him. He couldn't help smiling at her bullheadedness, risking the capricious wrath of the court on principle; no one could tell Rebecca what to do when she knew she was right. Joseph understood it was not because she was so sure she would get what she wanted from the court but rather that she refused to win on any terms but her own. She was stubborn but right, he reasoned, exactly like his own father.

During his first week on his own Joseph had removed the *kipa* from his head and the *tzitzit* fringes he wore under his shirt, shoving them to the back of a drawer stuffed with socks. He had watched the sun set, commencing his first Sabbath away from home, and flicked the lights on and off to see what would happen. It took several weeks for him to use a pencil or turn on a gas flame; until then he found excuses for why he had no need to write or cook on the Sabbath. He was still separating milk from meat and keeping *treyf* food out of his apartment so that, he hoped, his sons could one day eat a meal in his home.

The triumvirate of rabbis shuffled papers, sucked on their beards, sighed. The eldest of them spoke up, addressing no one in particular. "And you have done everything in your power to make peace between yourselves? You have made every effort at *shalom bayit* for the sake of those five boys?" And to Joseph, quietly, as if it were only the two of them in the courtroom together: "Surely this madness is behind you. A lovely wife, a lovely family. You are a religious man and a learned man. You know what the Torah says: a punishment of immense proportions." The fist behind Joseph's eye had swollen to the size of a small boulder and was pressing his nose, his ears, threatening to break through the top of his skull.

"Excuse me, Rabbi," said Rebecca's lawyer, "but this divorce was initiated by *my* client. Mr. Licht has no choice in the matter."

The rabbi stared hard at Rebecca's lawyer and then at Joseph, but said nothing. Joseph felt the rabbi was willing him to refuse to sign the *get*, urging him to use this divorce document to make his wife his prisoner. A ceiling fan whirred over Joseph's head, and he shuddered. He signed. The proceedings ended and they were divorced. The lawyers shook hands and chatted amicably while Joseph and Rebecca stood on opposite sides of the courtroom.

It was barely eleven o'clock when they emerged from the building together. "I'll call you about arranging a visit with the boys," Joseph told Rebecca. She stared blankly ahead. Divorced, severed, that was what they were now. He knew the reality: he was lonely, but free and unencumbered in Tel Aviv; she was saddled with five young boys and a father-in-law in a rural village. He looked closely at her, trying to see her from another man's perspective. Quietly attractive. Composed. Relaxed. The reality again: she looked haggard and defeated, hardened, a woman deprived of love. He knew this was his fault. He looked away.

Rebecca and the lawyers headed toward a nearby parking lot. Joseph's headache had lifted. He was feeling better and did not wish to return to his lonely apartment on this significant day. On an impulse he caught a taxi to the Central Bus Station. A bus would be leaving for Jerusalem in twenty minutes. He bought a ticket, then ambled past the merchants' stalls, fingering fabrics and dried fruit and cigarette lighters as he went. He stopped at a falafel stand to buy a cold drink.

The man at the register smacked the change into his palm and pulled him closer, meeting his face halfway across the counter. "Brighten up, pal," he said. "Tomorrow's another day." Joseph longed to tell him he had been divorced less than an hour earlier, but instead he pulled his hand away and shoved the straw into his mouth, sipping greedily at the sweet juice. He backed away from the stand, catching a brief glimpse of himself in a small mirror. Did he really look that glum, that miserable? He wound his way through the crowd and reached the bus just as it was beginning to load. In a few moments he was off.

How different this trip to Jerusalem felt, as the bus sped

past the tiny settlements and their furrowed fields. There was no longer the tingle of anticipation at seeing Yoel, no longer the clandestine pleasure of hopping a bus to a secret, passionate meeting. Joseph had not been to the capital since the day of their last tryst.

In Jerusalem he caught a taxi to Yoel's somber and imposing home on Elharizi Street, where his widow still lived. Again Joseph was taken with the steeply sloping roof, so incongruous with the flat-topped buildings surrounding it. He paid the driver and watched as the cab inched its way down the narrow street. He pushed the gate open, scanning the windows for signs of life. He thought he saw a face behind thin white curtains at an upstairs window, but he could not be sure. An aproned maid answered the door.

"I'm here to see Rebbetzin Rosenzweig," he stated, wondering if others also still used the honorific for the wife of a rabbi when addressing her.

"Madame is expecting you?" inquired the maid in a French North African accent.

Joseph stared past the maid at the long corridor and the winding marble staircase. "No," he said flatly. "But the matter is urgent."

"What is your name, and what do you want?" she asked bluntly.

"Joseph Licht. I've come . . ." He stopped short at the sight of the small, emaciated woman at the top of the staircase. She was a convergence of planes and angles. Her simple housedress gave her the look of a seamstress's mannequin. Her hair was tucked completely under a white turban, and a thin brown cigarette smoldered between her fingers.

Joseph pushed past the maid into the foyer. Yoel's widow

stared down at him, speechless. After a long moment she lifted the cigarette to her mouth, never taking her eyes from Joseph. She inhaled deeply and pushed the smoke out slowly. *"Dina, ammene Monsieur Licht au salon. Je viendrai."* Dina dutifully led Joseph into the salon without a word and shut the tall doors behind her as she left.

Joseph paced the formal room, stopping in the center to glance at the dark oil paintings, the deep, plush rugs, the heavy European furniture. He could imagine Yoel in this oppressive room, sipping cognac with guests and dreaming of escape. Thick curtains were drawn against the piercing Israeli sun.

She entered through a side door wearing a long robe pulled tightly around her. She was smoking another cigarette. Small pearl earrings peaked out from the edge of the turban.

She did not move close to Joseph, speaking from behind an overstuffed sofa. "My husband's lover and assassin. How odd to be meeting you."

Until this moment Joseph had not known what he would say, what pretense he would give for interrupting her peace. He had assumed she had never before heard his name and would believe he was a colleague, a student, an admirer of her dead husband.

"Don't look so surprised, Monsieur Licht. He told me all about you and your filthy relationship the day before he slashed his wrists." She lifted the cigarette to her mouth but did not inhale. "This has all been terribly hard on my children but, frankly, I'm glad he killed himself. What he did with you, the acts you . . ." She faltered, grasping the back of the sofa for support and taking a deep breath before continuing in a low, thin voice. "You and my husband, may his name be blotted from God's memory through eternity, you committed an unforgivable sin, you disobeyed God in the worst way and you squandered my husband's God-given gifts. You had your fun while my children and I must endure the damage every day of our lives."

Joseph's mind ran to Rebecca, tight-lipped that morning at the rabbinate. "I've come for a book your husband promised me," he said. The steady calm of his voice surprised him, gave him courage. "It's a small volume. I think I remember just where to find it on the shelves in your library."

The rebbetzin's eyes widened, the cigarette poised to drop burning ashes onto the patterned rug. "You have tremendous nerve coming here unannounced and asking me for anything at all. Your wife must be much more understanding than I about all this."

"We are divorced," he said without emotion, "as of this morning."

"She is divorced, I am widowed, and all of our children are orphans. You and my late husband, may his memory be wiped clean from the hearts of the pure, deserve an eternal hell together. Now go, Monsieur Licht, without your precious book, and do not return to this house, or I will tell my father you have been plaguing me and he will see to it that your punishment begins in this world, not the next."

Out on the street, in fresh air, Joseph found himself surprisingly lighthearted. He felt mischievous and daring; he'd even thought of sticking out his tongue at Yoel's widow or dashing to the library at the back of the house and stealing the book before bolting for the front door. While his colleagues at the university tried to make him feel better than he thought he ought to, she was the first person he had encountered who thought less of him than he did himself, and that liberated him somehow. He spent the rest of the afternoon aimlessly wandering the streets of Jerusalem, peering at his reflection in shop windows. He saw there a divorced man, a man once married but no longer, a bachelor again at thirty. From here, where?

The following Friday was Joseph's first outing with the boys, nearly three months since he had left home. He dipped into his meager savings to rent a car. His hands shook as he pulled away from the rental agency but as the roads opened up before him he relaxed, grateful for the wind that slapped and revived him. He had rarely been out of the city in all that time and now the smells of the farms he passed soothed him. About a mile before he reached Sde Hirsch the fist headache suddenly punched its way into his consciousness, but he banished it successfully and felt this was a good omen for the day.

Daniel, Ethan, and Noam were waiting for him at the bus stop at the entrance to the village. They wore sandals and white shirts and plaid shorts of different colors. All wore baseball caps, Noam's turned backward. He was eating cereal from a sandwich bag. A canteen hung against Daniel's hip and Ethan held a misshapen wooden box reverently in front of him with both hands. "Daddy, look!" he shouted as Joseph came around the car toward them. "I made this from Popsicle sticks!"

Joseph could barely stand, his legs were wobbling so badly. He leaned on the warm car for support but was choking on his tears and could not speak. Noam reached his hand up with an offering, one licked cornflake. Joseph tried to laugh, but a moan escaped instead. They had changed, his sons, in tiny, imperceptible ways; nothing he could pinpoint, just a graceful, gradual metamorphosis toward the young men they were becoming. He tried to study them all at once, to concentrate on each feature. But there was so much to look at and his eyes were blurring with tears. He breathed deeply and looked at the sky.

"Hey, what's that?" he cried, pointing at the top of the grain silo, relieved he had found his voice.

Daniel and Ethan turned to the silo but Noam stared at Joseph's outstretched finger. Ethan spoke up. "On Independence Day they lit it up. It says, 'Happy 28th Birthday, Israel' in different colored lights! Amos Kriegman made it with his dad." A small stab. What projects had Joseph carried out with his boys even when he had lived with them?

"I thought we would go for a ride, maybe over to the ruins at Caesarea."

"Oh," Daniel pouted. "We went there on a field trip last week. It was boring."

"Well," Joseph drawled, "we could take a tour of the winery in Zichron Yaakov. . . ."

Just then Miriam Wolloch—a childhood classmate of Joseph's—and her daughter Leah rounded the corner and nearly fell on top of Joseph and the boys. A breathless "Oh" flew out of her, then she took Leah firmly by the hand and marched on.

The Lichts could hear Leah as her mother pulled her down the street: "Mommy, why didn't you say hello . . . ? Mommy . . . ?"

Daniel scowled and spit, but his aim was off and saliva dribbled onto his shoe. Noam shoveled another handful of cornflakes into his mouth. "Daddy, why don't you live at home anymore?"

Joseph bent down on one knee and pulled Noam's face close to his. "You know, maybe I will have a cornflake after all," he said.

During the months that followed, Joseph invited the boys in different combinations—Daniel with the twins, or sons number one, three, and five—and he kept a large poster chart in his kitchen to keep track of whom he had seen and for how long. He was careful not to show partiality for any particular son, though he did take Daniel out once alone on Rebecca's insistence. The outings were mostly disasters: the boys would fight, they would embarrass him in public, they were untamed and uncontrollable. Daniel was uncommunicative while Ethan chattered and tried to monopolize Joseph's attention. Noam was easy, but the twins were still toddlers and they invariably grew tired and cranky. The mounting futility of these outings numbed Joseph, and more than once he wondered whether the boys would be better off without him. So when the head of his department, Professor Gabison, offered him a year's teaching position in Cleveland through a friend—"You're good, Joseph, very good. You've got a future here. But you've been through quite a bit this year and you need to recharge your batteries"—he imagined himself in a tiny apartment in the American Midwest with no reminders of Yoel, thought of the boys moving on with their lives, and accepted gratefully on the spot.

The academic year began much earlier in America than it did in Israel, and with so much to arrange Joseph felt it best to leave as soon as possible. He notified Rebecca of his plans by postcard, and asked her to allow him one last meeting with all five boys together, a picnic on the beach. His flight was leaving on a Wednesday and the day before, a Tuesday afternoon in late July, he took a bus north to a town close to Sde Hirsch carrying a huge hamper filled with sandwiches, fruit, sliced cheeses, frozen juices, and pastries, then hired a taxi to fetch the boys from the moshav. He was nervous, but the boys were so animated, laden with inflatable toys and plastic pails and sifters, that he could not help but laugh aloud.

There was no way for Joseph to describe that day to himself other than perfect. The sea was calm and warm and the boys were free to romp and push and splash. Only here, at the beach, could their noise and wild antics seem small and self-contained. He ventured out into deeper water with Daniel and Ethan and Noam and sat on the shore with the twins digging holes that flooded over again and again, leaving slick and shiny sand they loved to sink their feet into. Daniel led a campaign to bury Joseph under a mountain of dry sand but the digging wore them out and in the end they decided to bury only his legs. They took a walk to collect the shiniest, most colorful shells and sea glass in cloudy shades of green and gold.

At the end of the afternoon they sat in a huddle wrapped in towels and watched the blood-red sun inch its way closer to the horizon like a pomegranate too heavy for its branch. Joseph pointed out to sea. "That's where I'm going," he told them. "If you sail straight ahead, all the way to the other side of the Mediterranean Sea and then across the entire Atlantic Ocean, you'll find me there."

Noam squinted, looking for land. The twins, for once subdued, stared straight out to sea, looking at nothing. Ethan asked, "Can we visit you there, Daddy?" Daniel looked up to catch Joseph's answer.

"I'll only be gone a year," he said. One year. He calculated: one-eighth of Daniel's life, one-sixth of Ethan's, one-fifth of Noam's, and a third of the twins'. An eternity for them all, and longer than that for Joseph. It had seemed like such a good idea for everyone. He spread his arms around them, pulled the huddle closer. "I'll write you all the time, and send you pictures. And next summer I'll be home and we'll spend plenty of time at the beach together. This was lots of fun, wasn't it?"

When Rebecca came to fetch them he had already said his goodbyes. From a safe distance he watched them tumble into the station wagon and heard their cacophony of little voices shouting bits of information about their day to Rebecca. He lifted a hand to wave but caught only the sky's reflection in the car's window. Its tires spit pebbles and sand into the air as it sped away.

Professor Gabison had been right to send him away. Joseph saw this as soon as he got settled in Cleveland. Teaching kept him tremendously busy and focused his mind. He, a native speaker of Hebrew, was teaching English literature to English speakers. Obsessed with forcing the right sounds out of his mouth, he used exact and appropriate expressions, becoming more American than the Americans. He graciously allowed himself to be corrected, and quickly discovered this endeared him to colleagues and students alike. He learned to spread his a's wide and send them through the roof of his mouth like they did, picking up their shortcuts and saying *ornjuice* and *cotta cheese*, though he could never bring himself to tell people he taught *litterchure*. He was well liked and, as an outsider, nonthreatening.

Before he even landed in America Joseph had decided to

spend one hour every day on his children. This could be writing a letter to them or preparing bits and pieces of a package he would send. Sometimes he taped his voice, talking about what he was doing, what Cleveland was like, how much he missed them. He made up stories about the ducks in the lagoon at the art museum, described the view of the city and its lake and river from the Terminal Tower, collected veiny red and orange leaves from Sunday walks. He sent them maple sugar rosettes in the fall and red-and-white candy canes at Christmastime. In the spring he sent them Frisbees and baseball bats and tetherballs with instructions on how to play these exotic sports. And when the days grew longer and warmer he sent them a huge inflatable raft. He licked his lips for salt as he imagined them bobbing on the waves with him in just a few more months.

He received in return two envelopes from Sde Hirsch over the course of the year. The first held a bundle of letters and bills, with several drawings of farm animals by Ethan and the twins. No note. The second, in spring, was a packet of Passover greetings that his sons had prepared in school, all but Daniel. When Joseph telephoned, the older boys were usually out playing or too busy to come to the phone. The twins always wanted to talk, or at least breathe into the phone, but he only managed to catch the older three a few times.

Joseph set aside time that year for Yoel as well, time for reliving the relationship they had started to create, for imagining the press and warmth of his massive body. Joseph did not allocate an hour a day to Yoel as he did to his boys, but in fact he spent far more time than that with his dead lover, mostly in the quiet hours of the late night or early morning when he could shut out the day's intrusions and give himself

wholly to this one man much as he had when Yoel was still
alive. He hugged his pillow and tried touching himself the
way Yoel had, but those large prodding fingers had carried so
much curiosity and sadness and love that Joseph merely
made himself ache with desire for what he could not have.
He cried sometimes, but mostly he stared at the dark ceiling
in disbelief.

Often he tried to picture the life he could have had with
Yoel. He imagined them trekking the rim of a Norwegian
fjord, his hand cupped in Yoel's larger one, or buried in a
deep sofa, barely touching, each with his own book. Most of
his reveries included just the two of them, sealed in their own
hush-tone private world, but occasionally he would picture a
festive meal with their nine collective children, later joined
by daughters- and sons-in-law and hordes of grandchildren
turning pirouettes and playing tag willy-nilly around the
adults. They would all be charming, healthy, well behaved.
They would come to their two grandfathers for advice or a
gentle game of rummy, to share stories of classroom battles
and triumphs or to play a soulful tune on a violin. As grandfathers, Yoel and Joseph would listen patiently, offer wisdom,
and dole out silver coins or chocolates wrapped in colored
tinfoil. When the children all left, the house would reverber-
ate with their songs and laughter, so the grandfathers would
never feel lonely.

Still, he could never help imagining a different, less
attractive scenario of Yoel moving past fifty, sixty, seventy.
What would Joseph have found in him then? When would the
man he loved—the uneven stubble of his beard a sign of insou-
ciance and rebellion; the broad thickness of his chest, legs,
fingers testimony to his strength and solidity; the receding

hairline a sign of virility; the lines and creases in his face
the badges of a life of enriching experiences and meaning—
have become just an unkempt, fat, bald, wrinkled old man?
When he began to discover Yoel's foibles and flaws would he
then have weighed them against Rebecca's? Would his
heart's desire, the object of his love and longing, have turned
into heart grief? Would their small, self-contained world
have been able to sustain them? Since Yoel had opened new
worlds to Joseph, his death signaled the eradication of love,
the annihilation of intimacy, the end of hope.

Joseph had not been prepared for the physical pain he
felt at losing the boys. For years he had jealously watched
Rebecca, always pregnant or nursing, her whole body caught
up in creating and then providing for new life. His own body
was useless to each new baby that arrived. But now it was as
if each son had been severed from him like a limb, and he
ached at their absence.

The English Department threw him a farewell party at
the end of the spring semester and the university president
invited him to lunch and offered him a position whenever he
wished. But Joseph was desperate to return to Israel and
booked a flight that would launch him back into his life just
as soon as he could grade the last exam. He bought extra luggage to haul all the gifts he had purchased for the boys. True
to his word, Professor Gabison had an office and a course
load waiting for him.

From his first meeting with the boys Joseph recognized
the enormity of his mistake. Time and distance had wedged
him out of their lives; his gifts were paltry compensation,
like the offering of a barely tolerated cousin from overseas.
Moreover, the boys had grown spoiled and undisciplined.

Where once they had been boisterous, now they were impossibly loud and wild. They argued with one another, paid little attention to their father, and generally did exactly what they pleased. He felt he did not know these children and, because he had nothing to do with their upbringing, could not criticize or correct. When he wrote Rebecca about it, offering to help devise a way to raise them successfully in tandem, though apart, he got no response. He gave up planning outings and packing food. The boys were unhappy no matter where he took them. Joseph tried again to form groups conducive to good behavior, suspecting it was Daniel who was instigating and modeling this conduct. But even without his lead they were frightfully contentious. It became more and more difficult to convince them to do things with him, and Joseph took to inviting them one at a time for fear of losing them completely. He did not wish to plead for their company, knowing this would make them less inclined to spend time with him, but there seemed to be no other way. He paid large sums of money he did not have for tickets to sporting events that would entice them. He began to believe he had dreamt that perfect day at the beach.

Joseph could not have known it at the time—might have shot or drowned himself then, in the autumn of 1977, had he known—but he was beginning a slump of sorts that would last, with a few brief exceptions, until he met Pepe sixteen years later. His career would progress slowly, his well-researched but plodding articles rejected more often than not, his classroom demeanor under fire from semester to semester, his cantankerous and imperious nature increasingly an irritation to colleagues. His social life would never blossom during this period; he would shy away from potential friends and ignore admirers, preferring solitude and silence. He would have only three sexual liaisons, all errors of great magnitude in his eyes, a capitulation to weakness and an insult to the memory of his lovemaking with Yoel. And his relationships with his sons would dwindle and diminish until he could not remember ever really having been a father.

He would almost, but not entirely, forget what it was to love, or to be loved.

khol *(secular, common, profane; workaday)*

FRIDAY, MARCH 1, 1996

DANIEL STAGGERS TO THE bathroom, folds down the front of his pajama bottoms, and releases a swift and steady stream into the toilet. He has promised his roommate, Elyasaf, whose girlfriend has complained, that he will put the seat up before peeing, but once again, bleary-eyed and barely conscious, he has forgotten. The clothes he wore yesterday lie in a heap next to his bed. Inside the sweater is a flannel shirt and inside that a T-shirt, and Daniel slips all three together over his head, hopping up and down several times until they find their accustomed places on his body. His skullcap, small and soiled, falls from the right sleeve of the sweater and he clips it to his head, a tiny tent in the forest of his long, sandy curls. He zips up his trousers over his pajama bottoms and steps into work boots, which he will lace up at various stoplights en route to his first job. His morning prayers last fourteen minutes, including the time it takes to lay and then rewrap the *tefillin*. He adds enough milk to his coffee to cool it to the point where he can drink it straight down, leaves the empty cup in the sink with yesterday's dishes, and is out the door and in his van by seven o'clock.

There are four messages on his beeper and three on his cell-phone voice mail. Daniel reads and listens while driving, swerving to keep to his lane. Five of the messages are plumbing jobs that require his attention. The sixth is from his brother Ethan, asking how long before Shabbat he plans to arrive at their father's this evening. The last message is from his mother. "Ha toilet ist zatoom," she announces, and Daniel laughs aloud at her crazy mix of Hebrew, German, and English in one short sentence. He calls her immediately.

"What's wrong with the toilet, Ma?"

"Hello, Daniel. It's the toilet in Grandfather's cottage, all backed up. The water won't go down. I tried using the *Sauger* but nothing happened."

He figures she is referring to a plunger but does not bother to find out. "Tell Grandfather to use the bathroom in the big house for now. I'm on my way to a job but I'll come up to Sde Hirsch after that." Daniel curses as a taxi cuts in front of him.

"If you come early, I'll make you a big breakfast. How about an *oepfelroesti*? I've got lots of challah bread left from last Shabbat and all the right fruit."

"OK, Ma, sounds good. See you later." He remembers how Rebecca used to scoff at Polish mothers enticing their children to visit with a meal of home-cooked delicacies. Is she changing with age? Or is she just happy to get rid of aging leftovers, ever resourceful?

Daniel parks half on the sidewalk in front of the building he has been searching for. All at once he realizes he is only blocks away from his father's apartment. He has been there only once and found it too luxurious for his taste. And uncomfortable. Pepe, the painting of the nude man, the doorman who mocked him for ascending to the penthouse, unaware that he was a son and not a, a—it had been too much for him. Besides, he had nothing to say to his father, while Joseph had too much to say to him. The more his father expects of him the less Daniel is inclined to deliver, a pattern they established at least twenty years ago.

Daniel will turn twenty-eight a few weeks after this family reunion. He is earning a very handsome living now, a fact he chooses not to share with anyone, especially his father. He does not want to ruin his reputation as the family's greatest underachiever, refuses to ignite his father's hopes for him. Nor does he admit to the odd happiness that has come to him in such a surprising fashion: the joy of fixing things, the comfort of routine, the bustle of city life. Daniel likes paying house calls much more than he thought he would. He had never thought himself curious about other people's lives, but the more he gains admittance to their kitchens and bathrooms, the more he wants to know about them. He enjoys, too, the attention of the women he finds in those kitchens and bathrooms. They invite him for coffee, even bake him a cake or cookies while he is working; sometimes they touch him when his head is wedged under a sink and his legs are sticking out, vulnerable. One teenager in a particularly swanky building in north Tel Aviv felt compelled to take a bath while Daniel was replacing the bidet.

He ascends to the fourth floor, where he is greeted by a thin, very dark young woman—Persian or Yemenite, he believes. Her hair is raven black and falls to her shoulders.

He cannot tell if she is eighteen or twenty-eight. He does not know whether she is the lady of the house or the daughter or the hired help. She offers no clues.

The malfunctioning dishwasher proves a cinch to fix. The dark young woman flits in and out of the kitchen while Daniel tinkers. In and out, in and out, with the speed and silence of a sparrow. He finds himself slowing down, checking his work, tightening bolts, taking all precautions. He is lingering in spite of his heavy workload and the unexpected trip north to fix his grandfather's toilet. He does not know if this is because he wants to find a way to talk to her or because he wishes to make very sure she will have no additional plumbing problems. He wants to ease the burden of her life.

Eventually Daniel cannot find anything more to check. He stands to his full height and in his work boots he feels too large for this kitchen and the young woman it contains.

"Please don't go yet," she chirps from across the room. In an instant she is in front of him, he with his back up against the dishwasher. Indian. He recognizes the accent now, the rich brown of her lips.

She reaches up and caresses his chin, cupping her hand and moving it along his jawbone. He closes his eyes, waiting for himself to pull away and quite surprised at himself when he does not. She is using both hands now, gently massaging his shoulders and chest, and he leans in to catch her scent. Daniel's eyes spring open when she kisses his lips, but her own eyes are closed; there is no gaze to meet. He closes his eyes again, acquiescing. She settles her cheek against his chest and his feet seem to take root, right there in front of the dishwasher. They breathe together, slow and quiet.

Down in the van, out of sight of the apartment, after a wordless parting, he shreds her bill and voids the copy.

* * *

On mornings like these, when he awaits the convoy of jeeps and armored vehicles that will ferry him back across the border into Israel, Ethan feels a tug of anxious energy. He has learned, over the course of these many months that have sprawled out across a year, that his apprehension has little to do with the dangerous beauty of the journey ahead of him, sixteen short kilometers of roads that float and sink through the deep valleys and craggy mountains and tiny, silent villages of southern Lebanon, which provide a hundred thousand perfect hiding places from which to lob a Molotov cocktail or aim a machine gun. He has an officer's faith in the intelligence and might of the Israel Defense Forces and a fatalist's resignation to luck and destiny. Nor does it have anything to do with the competence of the command of his first lieutenant, Guy, who will be in charge during his three-day leave. His anxiety today is not even about the reunion weekend with his father and brothers that has crowded into his waking thoughts these past weeks. He is simply afraid of missing something—that undefined, unscheduled event he has prepared himself and his soldiers for during endless hours of drills and exercises and marches and simulations.

There is little to pack or prepare. Ethan's two lives—military and civilian—have almost nothing to do with one another and, aside from dirty clothes for washing, very few objects make the crossover with him: a book, a pair of *tefillin*, a wallet. He sheds his everyday uniform, shoving it into his laundry sack, and dons his dress uniform. His two lieutenant's bars gleam on the shoulder. He idly wonders how long it will take to gain the third, when he will be made a captain.

He managed to sleep this morning for two hours, right here on the cot in his office, under a plastic-covered map that shows every building and every tree in his sector. As commanding officer of this outpost he cannot sleep in the barracks with his hundred or so men, so he spends his nights in their company awake, visiting their guard posts, ostensibly offering help in keeping alert during the long, dark night hours but really in search of their aid in staving off his own deep and hungry loneliness.

Most of his men have girlfriends back home or posted elsewhere in the army. During the day they grab precious free moments to phone their families, offering quick reassurances that they were far away from whatever recent attack their parents saw on the news. But nighttime is for phoning the girlfriends, who are resigned to receiving calls at two, three or four o'clock in the morning. He tries not to listen to their quiet proclamations of love or to the indiscreet boys who tell their girls how and where they will touch them on their next leave. Ethan prefers to catch their tone, that mix of machismo and tenderness and prayer that floats above them like static heat. At those quiet moments when the guns are still and the jeeps are grounded for the night and the phone does not ring and the sirens are silent, and the only noise is a young man blowing bubbles of love through a phone line to a young woman in a nightgown with sleep in her eyes, then Ethan leans back and laps at the air like a dog, inhaling her soft and powdered love like a sprinkling of angel dust. He thinks this must be the taste of heaven.

Ethan's hair is quite straight, the sand color of Daniel's but without a single one of Daniel's curls, and it has thinned considerably in the last year or two. In fact, he is the only Licht man—including his four brothers, his father, and even his ninety-year-old grandfather—to be developing a bald spot. His best feature is his full and sensuous lips.

Ethan has gray eyes the color of a winter sky and a nose that seems to come from an earlier generation—narrow and a tad hooked. He is stouter than his brothers, fuller, with the look of a scrappy but bighearted guy. He has a quick smile that fades even quicker, and his eyes rarely smile along with his mouth. His two upper front teeth are whiter than the others; they are false, the real ones sacrificed to the side of a swimming pool when he was twelve. He is also missing the tip of his left pinkie, the result of a mishap with a piece of rusting but sharp farm equipment (an imperfection that kept him out of a certain crack army unit), and he has a scar that runs a parallel course to the fine line of hair on his belly— from a ruptured appendix that nearly killed him at fourteen. He has also endured major knee surgery and a tonsillectomy and worn braces on his legs to correct a severe orthopedic disorder. As a child he was forever falling and tripping and bruising and cutting himself, so that there was one first-aid kit for the entire family and another just for Ethan. Squeezed in so tightly in the three-year spread between first-born Daniel and the irresistible Noam, getting hurt often was Ethan's best bet for attention.

Ethan was sent to officer training school earlier than usual. He signed on for an extra two years, and then more. He has fallen into an army career without really ever deciding to do so. He knows about the army benefits—medical, pension—and mentions them when anyone questions him about his future, because it would be impossible to explain that he stays because the army is the first thing he has fully understood in his life. He loves the camaraderie, the respect he has earned. He loves the ease of wearing the same uniform day after day, the advancement and citations he has received. He loves the army's lack of color, the way it throbs and swaggers. If he stays much longer they will send him to study at university, but he wishes he could keep doing what he is doing now forever.

At 2:00 a.m. he had gone to keep Asher company. He could hear the sergeant from several feet away, before he reached the guard post, since Asher was noisily cracking sunflower seeds in his teeth and deftly sucking out the meat while spitting the shells onto the floor.

"That's quite a pile you've built up there," Ethan said, pointing to a mound of shells that reached the laces on his boots.

"Nothing else to do here." Asher did not move his eyes from the empty dark in front of him. All of Ethan's soldier's have learned to talk, listen, crack seeds, or pee while giving their full attention to the scenery ahead, even and especially at night, when a terrorist could touch the end of your M16 before you even knew he was there.

Ethan stared ahead for a while into the blackness with his soldier. Nothing stirred. Asher moved his helmet back to scratch his scalp, then tugged at his crotch. "I think I've got lice or some skin disease. Can't stop scratching." He continued to rub himself violently for several minutes.

"What you need is a good shower."

"That's easy for you to say. You're the one leaving in a

few hours." Asher stopped scratching, munched a few seeds. "Got any special plans?"

Ethan threw his head back to catch sight of a spray of stars. The words came out clipped from his stretched throat. "My father's having a fiftieth birthday party for himself, a reunion at his place in Tel Aviv. All my brothers'll be there." He thought about his sister-in-law, Batya, but said nothing.

"You know," Ethan said, looking down at Asher, "my dad left home when I was about six. Left my mom with five boys under the age of eight. It was hell on her, God love her, but I think it's what made me a good soldier."

Asher looked up at him then, trying to gauge whether his CO was serious. When he had confirmed Ethan was, he looked straight out again into the darkness.

"No, really, Asher. Without a father, a male role model, I had to be my own man of the house. I learned to take responsibility at an early age, I became a leader. And it just goes to show that you can overcome nearly any obstacle if you know how to turn it around to your own advantage."

Asher did not say a word. He cracked a few more seeds, spit the shells onto the pile. Finally he stood up, unbuttoned his trousers, and fished his penis out for a long piss, his eyes all the while fixed on the middle distance. "Take this, you Hezbollah shits!" he shouted into the darkness and let fly a noisy fart.

It is after nine o'clock and the convoy of jeeps is ready to depart. Ethan takes a last look around the office, passes a set of keys to his second in command, and begins the slow journey back to Israel, where people are expecting him.

* * *

Rebecca has a new morning ritual these past few weeks: She kneads her belly with the heel of her hand, low, where the babies once grew. How odd to feel a swell there again! She grins dreamily, recalling the pregnancies she enjoyed so much, even with the twins, when her stomach pushed forward so far she thought it might crack and ooze like an overripe melon, worried that one day she might find those babies tumbling out the front of her without warning, ripping through her clothes and rolling down her legs.

Now her skin is taut and shiny again but shapeless. Doughy. That is what they call it in Hebrew: *batzeket*, from the same root as the word for dough. Her English dictionary calls it an edema, which she thinks would make a pretty name for a girl. She once heard of a baby called Placenta, so why not Edema? Still she prefers the Hebrew, like some slow-baking cinnamon *kuchen* rising and swelling between her vital organs. She had felt that dough from the outside on her neighbor, Penina Belkin, through long months of nursing her, watching it swell until it seemed to swallow Penina's insides altogether. Now Rebecca is getting to know her own *batzeket*, from within. Loose, thick, wobbly. She kneads and prods, searching for its boundaries. Where does it begin, where does it end? What is it hiding?

Mostly Rebecca is neither frightened nor angered by her edema. In the morning she takes an interest but lets it slip her mind until bedtime, when she explores the contours again. This dough pouch is still her secret. She has resisted making an appointment with the new village doctor, a gaunt young man with the wild hair of a clown's wig. She has not told her father-in-law or any of her sons. She did not mention it to her mother, Esther, during their weekly phone call. She would not be able to stand her mother's bustling efficiency just now, as Esther would certainly catch the first Tel Aviv–bound flight from Zurich upon hearing such news. Rebecca wishes to become acquainted with her *batzeket* quietly, alone.

In one sense she is almost grateful for the soft and shapeless bubble; it has brought sharp focus to her immediate plans or, rather, has awakened her to possibilities she had stuffed away like the odds and ends she finds around her house, hidden in old coffee tins or behind books on high shelves or in the rickety old shed in the garden. She wishes to visit her childhood friend Rosa, who lives now in Vancouver. She resolves to buy the silk scarf, wild with jungle colors and shapes, that she saw in town last week. She wants not to make a single preparation for the upcoming Passover holiday, then to close up her house and go away for the entire week.

Rebecca will be busy today, the Jewish housewife's Friday busy, but even more so with Ethan unexpectedly in the house (now asleep for a few hours in his old room) and Daniel on his way from Tel Aviv to fix the toilet in his grandfather's cottage. As always, she has no list of chores. They sprout throughout the day and she hacks away at them as they catch her attention: collect eggs from the coop, iron Manfred's white Sabbath shirt, prepare the usual meals, bake the usual cake. She notices half an aging loaf of challah on the bread board and remembers her promise to whip up an *oepfelroesti* for Daniel and Ethan, so she rips it into thick chunks and leaves them to soak in egg.

With Penina it started in the ovaries, but little bits and pieces broke off and floated skyward like balloons, bumping finally into the top of her skull and settling in to her brain. She lost her mind, then her speech, then her life. Rebecca squeezes a chunk of sopping bread and wonders down what path her own *batzeket* will propel her.

The screen door to the back porch creaks open and Daniel lumbers in, ramming his toolbox into the metal wash-basin. The chicken coop behind the house comes alive with an indignant clamor, but to Rebecca the birds' cackling seems like laughter at Daniel's clumsiness.

"Good morning, son. Eat first or work first?" Rebecca rinses the slimy yolk from her hands, dries them on a tea towel slung over a chair, and cuffs her eldest son on the cheek. Just recently Daniel has been finding opportunities to talk with her, as candidly as he is capable of, and she hopes this will be such an occasion.

He stops to consider the question, halfway into the kitchen from the porch. His eyes shift but focus on nothing. She is free to stare at him now, since she knows he will not notice. It fascinates her to be able to look at this son—only this son—and see him at two years old, at five, at eleven. Nothing has changed—not his round, sad eyes or his slow smile or his tangled muss of curly hair. She waits patiently while he finishes consulting with his stomach.

"I'm not quite hungry yet. I'll go over to Grandfather's first." All at once Daniel's cell phone rings and his beeper chirps, creating an unusual din in Rebecca's crowded kitchen. Her face contorts at the intrusion of these foreign sounds in her farmhouse, but Daniel ignores them. "Have you got pow-dered sugar for the *oepfelroesti*?" he asks on his way back out the porch door.

"Of course!" she calls after him, adding, "Be gentle with Opa, he's not quite been himself lately." She considers telling Daniel about yesterday's episode, how she spotted Manfred wandering dazed out back behind the house, his trousers unbuttoned, his jaw slack, drool spilling from his mouth, and how she sat beside him in the emergency room, watching him slip from lucidity to befuddlement and back again until the doctor said there was nothing physically wrong with him and sent him home. But Daniel is out of earshot and she merely watches as he treads heavily through the back garden, weighed down by too much equipment. He has always been her biggest mystery, right from babyhood. She assumed they would all be like him: shy and quiet, filled with secrets, self-sufficient. But they were not. The others chattered and demanded her attention.

When she and Joseph were first married they liked to imagine filling this quiet old farmhouse with babies. A dozen, fifteen, as many as they could. There would be legions of them. The whole village would brim over with little Lichts. They would add rooms to the house and stack beds in each room and the children would share clothing and toys and chores. He had brought her an article about a family whose first seven children had raised their next seven children, which seemed quite enchanting at the time to Joseph and Rebecca, each of whom had grown up in a home with no siblings.

Thus it was no surprise to them at all when Rebecca became pregnant within months of their marriage. She felt exceedingly healthy and exuded a quiet contentment that grew with each passing day. She especially loved Joseph's excitement, how he talked and sang to her burgeoning belly every night and told their unborn baby stories, which he would repeat each time he planted a new son in her womb. And when at the end of labor with Daniel she lay panting and spent on the birthing table and said it had all been love-ly but that next time they would try this or that differently, it was clear that what she loved the most and did the best was growing babies.

Though Joseph could be a difficult husband, Rebecca saw nothing but promise in his fathering. He adored the boys as babies, tossing them in the air or hanging them from tree branches, and when the older three were toddlers he thought nothing of rolling on the floor with them for half an hour, fascinated by their incoherent gurgling and their chunky, compact bodies.

But he grew increasingly preoccupied and testy, and his patience waned as the boys stepped out of babyhood. Rebecca had felt her fourth pregnancy was ill-timed—indeed, a surprise, a result of their first lovemaking in many months—and when she discovered she was carrying twins she became doubly dismayed. But what frightened her most was the kernel of certain knowledge she felt one day in the depths of her belly, as solid and real as a tumor, that this would be her last pregnancy, that her womb would close before she had even reached thirty. She wept bitterly then, but never again.

When Ethan wanders into the kitchen fastening his skullcap to his thinning hair with a clip, he finds his mother in the center of the room, staring off at nothing, one hand on her belly and the other poised above a bowl of bread chunks floating in egg.

"Mom?" he half whispers, careful not to startle her.

"Oh, Ethan," she says breathlessly, "why are you up already?"

"Well, I'm glad you're so happy to see me." Ethan tries to say this lightly, but fails.

Rebecca takes his face in both hands, bending his head and kissing him awkwardly on the forehead. "I know how little sleep you get up there in Lebanon and I hoped you'd stay in bed for a few hours more to catch up. You are worried about the base? There was no talk of Lebanon on the morning news."

Ethan's mind races to his outpost and back. He wonders if he has missed something important, something that would not as yet have reached the media. "Mom, what were you thinking when I came into the kitchen?"

It has come early this time, she thinks, this question he always asks. Why, she wonders, does this son want so much to climb inside her fuzzy old head? She eyes her kitchen, as if in search of an answer inside one of the cupboards. For years all the boys, except perhaps Noam, tried to get her to redo this room—the shabbiest, least comfortable, and most used space in the house—but Rebecca had become more and more stubborn about it with time. All at once she can see what they had been talking about: the flaking paint and the dented cabinets, the torn window screens and the crazy mix of colors and patterns; it made her head, her whole body feel tired and heavy.

"I was just trying to decide whether to start breakfast yet, or maybe to begin boiling the chicken for your grandfather's Shabbat meal. It's hard to know how long he'll be over there."

"Grandfather?"

"No, no. Daniel. He's come to fix Grandfather's toilet."

"Daniel's here now?"

She knows Ethan is doubly disappointed, having failed

to coax a deep and meaningful reverie from her and cheated out of a morning with his mother all to himself. He falls into a chair at the kitchen table. Rebecca fills a teakettle with tap water and lights the gas flame. Just as she is about to put the kettle on the burner she notices Ethan's eyes on her stomach. He opens his mouth. She sees the question forming in his mind and suddenly she knows, with a feeling of sadness and regret, that her secret will be short lived.

She chooses a voice that is brighter and cheerier than she feels to cut him off. "Yehoshua Belkin brought by some fresh cream last night, very thick, and I've bought myself some good coffee instead of that powdered instant, so we're going to have a real treat."

Daniel stomps onto the porch and throws open the kitchen door before Ethan can frame his question. "Mom, I need some rags. . . ." He stops just inside the door when he catches sight of his brother. "Hey, Ethan!" he cries heartily. Ethan does not rise from his chair but they slap hands in the air and hold on to one another for several moments. "When did you get in? I didn't see your car."

"My driver brought me. He'll bring the car back later this afternoon."

"Your timing is wonderful, Daniel," says Rebecca. "The kettle is just boiling and I'm making us all a nice cup of coffee. Sit down for a moment."

Rebecca sprinkles cinnamon onto the cream floating atop the coffee and hands him the first mug. Daniel accepts it but backs toward the door. "I've got a mess over at Grandfather's. Do you have some old rags I can use?"

She points to a box of old cloth scraps on the porch.

Daniel stoops and picks up the whole carton with one hand, the steaming mug still in his other. "See you both soon," he calls over his shoulder on his way out the porch door.

Rebecca sets a mug down in front of Ethan. She leaves her own on the counter and is on her way to her bedroom before he can remember to ask what is on his mind.

*   *   *

Despite foul weather and disturbing dreams, Joseph's spirits are high this morning. Today he performs only some of his morning toilette, skipping even the ritual shave and shower. Without regret he will stain his hands with floor wax and splatter himself with cooking grease. Besides, Pepe is gone and no stray caller could penetrate this fortified building. Except for an early-morning outing to the shuk for last-minute fresh produce Joseph will spend the day blissfully, busily alone. He throws on a powder blue jogging suit and sneakers, and has just buzzed the doormen to hail a cab for him when the phone rings. He does not answer, fearing a cancellation, a stray son with a change of heart. He listens as the call is picked up by the answering machine.

"*Bom día, querido!*" It is Pepe shouting down the line from Rio. Joseph considers ignoring him and heading out the door, then on an impulse grabs the receiver.

"Aha, Joseph, you were afraid I was one of the boys, eh? Didn't want bad news?"

Pepe's voice is nearly drowned out by the ferocious din of revelers. Before Joseph can respond, a different voice slobbers a tune into his ear: "She loves you blah, blah, blah."

Pepe is on the line again. "Don't mind these crazy drunken

fools. What a Carnaval this year! People are wilder than ever. Or maybe I'm just not in the swing anymore. Do you think I'm an old man already?"

"Younger than springtime, are you, gayer than everybody . . ." Before the line goes dead, the slobberer's voice erupts into a throaty laugh, or perhaps he is choking. For a moment Joseph does not replace the receiver and considers quickly slipping out the front door, but after giving it a second thought he returns the receiver to its cradle. A minute later, the phone rings again.

"I'm up in my room. Now you can hear me?" Pepe's tone is conciliatory, amorous. He would be sliding his coarse and stubby fingers beneath the cotton cloth of Joseph's sweat suit if he were at home now.

Joseph relaxes. He acquiesces. After all, Pepe is far away. "I hear you fine, Pepinho. How are you, my love?"

"Ah, there's my Josi." Pepe is clearly pleased. "I met with Carolina yesterday. She wants to visit us in Israel, and meet you. I'm getting to like her a lot; she's special. Clever and sexy together. Maybe one of your boys will like to marry her and then you and I become family!" He breaks into a leering laughter that Joseph recognizes, and detests.

Pepe's newfound grown daughter Carolina is pretty, that Joseph knows from the photograph in the living room. Pepe claims no memory of her mother's looks, but he is certain she was a dancer at a club he frequented and that she must have seduced him during one of his notorious drunken stupors. Joseph supposes that Noam is the only one of his sons who would dare fall for a non-Jewish girl, and he resolves they will never meet.

"I see you're in a rare mood. Being in Rio certainly does

relax you. You're never this much fun at home." Joseph is careful to soften the edges of his voice, since Pepe has the uncanny ability to pick up his slightest nuances, both the ones Joseph wishes to hide and those he wants to flaunt. Many times Pepe has tapped into his mood, dredging up grudges and hardened lumps of anger long before Joseph has been prepared to expose them.

But Pepe is oblivious to Joseph's long-distance jabs. "Ah, Josi-meu, and how are your big preparations coming along? I'll bet the table is set and all the food is cooked and you've even put the Shabbat candles into their holders. Right? Are all those luscious boys of yours still planning to come? Nobody's backed out?"

Luscious. The word chokes Joseph with rage. He feels he could slap Pepe senseless or worse: scratch blood to the surface of his age-spotted skin, tear his shriveled cock from its root, wrench his mocking eyes from their sockets, sever the offending tongue from his mouth. This is not Pepe's first infraction or even his worst—there's the way he embraces Noam or holds Ethan's hand in a long handshake, the way he appraises the boys' bodies when he thinks no one is watching, his lewd jokes, and sexual innuendos—but it enrages Joseph nonetheless. He speaks in a tight, controlled voice. "There is a lot I still have to do today, but I'll manage. And, yes, I believe they're all coming, even Gidi's wife."

"Good, good. Anyway, I'm calling to say happy birthday to you and to tell you you'll find your gift in the medicine cabinet, behind the laxatives."

Joseph takes a long, deep breath, steadying himself. "Thank you for remembering," he says as sweetly as he can. For a long moment after hanging up, he cannot recall what it was he was about to do. But he is certain that the medicine cabinet is not on his list this morning and he resolves to avoid looking for his gift.

He acknowledges to himself that what he told Pepe was not entirely true: he has extended invitations to all his sons, but not a one has quite exactly, precisely said he was coming. To this he is accustomed—their avoidance, the way they shift their eyes away from his own, the hooded hurt that still lingers. But he knows, too, to read around and under their words and their expressions, to pick up clues over the telephone lines. He is nearly certain they have been convincing one another, as always, in tight collusion, and that they will all arrive before the Sabbath begins that afternoon.

He wonders for the thousandth time how this Pepe, a man of crude appetites and unsavory business practices, is able to be so maddening and so disarmingly charming at the same time, how he has a knack for selecting just the present or thinking of just the idea. On the anniversary of their first year together Pepe presented Joseph with dress-circle tickets to an opera in Milan. On Joseph's birthday that year Pepe arranged to fill every room of the apartment with sumptuous flower arrangements that took three delivery boys more than an hour to install. Concerts, a catered picnic, a private cooking lesson with a master chef, a champagne breakfast for forty guests, the theater festival at Edinburgh, the races at Ascot, tennis at Wimbledon, opera at Bayreuth—Pepe consistently provides the most exquisite of temporal pleasures. To Joseph they blend and fold together like a sweet batter of memories, one long whorl of eating, drinking, spectating. Short, pithy speeches; commissioned cantatas; frothing glasses raised in toasts; well-dressed friends; undressed friends. Teeth, tongues, gesticulating hands. So much talking! So much laughing! So much singing!

Several weeks after they first met, Pepe invited Joseph to Paris, his litmus test for new loves. Where else could he impress a guest with his knowledge and cosmopolitan ease and provide such romantic, elegant surroundings? Besides, he felt it was far less complicated to treat a new friend to a long weekend in Paris than to risk a potential entanglement on home territory.

On their third day of steady gray rain Pepe brought Joseph to a resplendent cookware shop in Les Halles, right in the shadow of the church of Saint-Eustache. Joseph was still grappling with the fact that every shopkeeper, clerk, and maître d' they had encountered seemed to know Pepe. Who had accompanied him on all his previous junkets, Joseph wondered? Shopping for kitchen appliances proved strange, much stranger than picking out a bathing suit for Joseph, as they had done the day before, stranger still than receiving breakfast from a sallow young bellhop in the enormous hotel bed fitted with silk sheets. Kitchenware implied domestic intimacy; Joseph did not understand what Pepe meant in ushering him to this particular shop. He had no idea what Pepe had in his own kitchen. Whose kitchen were they out-fitting? Joseph's own tiny kitchenette, or a large, gleaming room they would share one day, where pots and pans would hang from hooks and stacks of china would rest comfortably behind panes of glass? Pepe recommended whisks, basters, sieves, funnels, tongs, spatulas, ladles, and other more com-plicated appliances that required explanations and demon-strations. They had the whole lot shipped back to Israel; Pepe supplied his own mailing address. "But you are the one who will be using them," he told Joseph, with a wink to the matronly shopkeeper.

When the doorman rings to announce—less politely than Joseph would like—that a taxi has been waiting for his descent for several long minutes, Joseph takes a quick look at himself in the mirror beside the door, throws a coat over his arm, and puts the apartment and his memories behind him and heads for the market.

*   *   *

After changing into a roomy housedress and a knitted sweater pulled loose with age and use, Rebecca sneaks out the front of the house as quietly as possible, careful not to let the screen door slam shut. She heads around to the back of the property toward Grandfather's cottage, but stops at the old shed, where she thinks she may have mislaid her gardening gloves. The heavy wooden door needs coaxing, but Rebecca knows all the secrets of this farm; she slips her foot into the wide gap between the cement floor and the bottom of the door and lifts it slightly before pushing it open.

The air is close in the shed, and she hears paws scampering as her eyes adjust to the dim light. Sixty years of moshav living are buried here, a history in miniature of the State of Israel: wire cots provided to new immigrants on their first nights in the country; a mesh coop for babies, where Rebecca could leave the boys in the fresh air without worrying about mosquitoes or bees or stray cats; a rocking horse sent by Joseph's aunt Lotte, who escaped to America before the war and lives there still; doorless armoires and cane chairs with no seats; a pile of waterlogged mattresses; an old radio the size of a child's coffin; and several generations of farm equipment, from milking machines to feed grinders to chick incubators. Rebecca feels more at home in this small, dark, overcrowded room than anywhere else in the world, and it is here that a suffocating despair suddenly squeezes at her chest. For the first time in as long as she can remember she is terrified. Not for her boys, out there colliding with life, accruing bruises and scars; not for her father-in-law or for her mother, both reaching great old age and inevitable decline; certainly not for Joseph, whom she once pitied for turning his back on so much love: now, at the thought of her own futureless future, she is terrified for herself. Amid the discarded junk of the cramped shed she pictures scalpels and hospital gowns, oxygen machines and body scanners. She pictures pain so sharp it sears her belly and she doubles over, her breathing ragged. She pictures nausea and fatigue. She pictures herself surrounded by her sons, and she pictures her own loneliness. But before she can picture her death she straightens herself to her full height, unfurls her fists, breathes. She pushes the unwanted images away, tries to remember what it was that brought her to the shed, and casts about for her gardening gloves. She remembers that the men are waiting for her, and her gloves are nowhere in sight, so she backs out of the shed and picks her way through the sand and weeds to Grandfather's cottage, wiping away her anxiety with the back of her hand.

She finds Daniel on his knees in front of the toilet, a metal coil plunged deep into the bowl. Grandfather is sitting on a stool in the corner, scribbling on a small pad of paper.

"Then you divide the whole sum in half and you get the year of your birth. So let's see. Two into one hundred and thirty-six. Yes. So, you were born in '68, no? Am I right?"

Grandfather looks first to Daniel's stooped back then to Rebecca for confirmation. *"Guten morgen, Rebecca. Das ist richtig, ya—1968?"*

She knows this trick of his. He has performed it on every human being whose birthday Rebecca can recall. He has guessed her mother's birth year, her friend Rosa's, all of her cousins'. Unlike so many other things, it has never failed him. "Yes, Opa, Daniel was born in 1968."

From the toilet comes the sound of a loud burp. "There we go," says Daniel, standing. The metal coil dredges up a huge wad of muck, which Daniel lifts carefully to a bucket. He flushes and the water runs freely. "Just overstuffed," he says to his mother. He crouches down in front of his grandfather and says in a near shout, "Opa, you can't put so much toilet paper into the bowl at one time. You'll clog up this old toilet again and again, so just flush *before* you're finished and then again when you're all done."

Grandfather stands up so abruptly he nearly knocks Daniel backward. Still, he grabs his grandson's arm to steady himself. Rebecca sees he is insulted but she is not sure by what. Perhaps it is Daniel's manner of speaking to him, as if to a child; perhaps he is embarrassed by Daniel's forthrightness, talking of private matters so candidly. Rebecca knows he will never agree to waste that much water by flushing twice. Maybe he is even a bit peeved that Daniel has not acknowledged the birth-year trick.

She motions to Daniel to gather his tools and go straight back to the house. She follows Grandfather to his kitchen, where she finds him rinsing a bowl in the sink. "Opa?" she calls lightly to him from behind. She notices for the first time the way his head has begun to sink beneath the horizon of his shoulders, how soon he and she will be of equal height. He does not turn around or acknowledge her in any way.

At the very spot on which she is standing now, Rebecca began her life in Israel, in this cottage that was once a cow shed, one long narrow room with a kitchen carved out of one end and a bathroom out of the other. She had thrown herself into making it a home: she sewed curtains and painted an old armoire she had found lying in deep weeds and poured stones to make a path through the dirt to the main house and planted a small vegetable garden. She tried some of her mother's recipes, but they were complicated and often required some ingredient she could not find at the village greengrocer's, so she learned from her neighbor Penina instead. She sent Joseph off to the university each morning in a freshly ironed shirt and shoes she polished and buffed to a deep, rich glow. Each day she cooked him a full breakfast, packed him sandwiches and fruit and home-baked pastries, and had a hot meat meal on the table when he returned in the evening.

She tries to remember now, as she watches her father-in-law's stooped back at the kitchen sink, whether she was happy then. She was in Israel, away from her mother, out of earshot of the Swiss who called her "Jewish swine" from behind cheerful window gardens, far removed from the grasp of spindly Jewish diamond merchants who wanted her hand in marriage. She was in Eretz Israel; she was living the Zionist dream; she had become a full-fledged member of her people, had become part of a history that was being written as she lived it. It was exhilaration she must have felt back then, and every shirt she ironed or meal she cooked was her own contribution to the building of this land and this people.

So when, she wonders, did the awe and pride and excitement turn to drudgery? How long did it take her to ask herself whether she had made a mistake by marrying this second cousin of hers, this man who became more of a stranger the longer they were married? When he had visited Switzerland she had been roused by his attentiveness, his sensitivity, and certainly by the flow of his prattle, the quickness of his mind, his ability to seize an idea or an image and dance it until it revealed its every curve and angle. He was fire and wind compared to the cool European boys she had known in Zurich, the sons of merchants or Holocaust survivors from the east, or pale Swiss Jews too long inbred. But in Israel he became absorbed in his studies, and by winter their routines were long established, patterns they would retain until their last day together. It became her responsibility to maintain the house, cater to his father (cook meals, do housework, help with the farm chores, be an attentive audience for his tirades), and make sure that Joseph never wanted for anything and could therefore devote his entire mind and energies to studying English language and literature.

At night they dined together, though Rebecca spent much of the meal jumping up to remove a boiling pot from the stove or fetch him a napkin or a cold drink or the saltshaker. She became increasingly nervous that she might forget something or spill something or burn something, so that even when he was sharing an opinion about a story he had read or explaining a theory he had developed, she found herself scanning the small kitchen in search of potential disaster.

In bed at night she would lie patiently in a flannel night-gown under a heavy comforter waiting for Joseph to emerge from the bathroom. They would share the light from a small lamp and lie reading until Joseph would sigh, slip a bookmark between the pages, and lean over to kiss her on the forehead. On occasion, mostly in the predawn hours, when the farmers were up milking their cows, and one-eyed Litovsky was using a long-handled paddle to slide the first loaves of the day into a roaring stone oven just down the road from them, they might make love. They would fumble with their pajamas but they would find one another under the sheets and their stomachs would make smacking noises as skin met skin and she would feel hopeful about him, feel that maybe she would, over time, find the softer, more vulnerable side to her husband.

During their years in America, while Joseph was studying and then completing his dissertation, Rebecca found life even harder. There were two toddlers and a baby when they left Israel and two more, the twins, by the time they returned. Joseph's moods were unbearable and the small flat in Cambridge felt like a broom closet when he was around. She missed her cottage and her garden, the cackling from the chicken coop, the smell of baking bread from Litovsky's ovens and the heavy perfume of orange blossoms in winter. She longed for sunshine and space, for a place where her laundry and her children would fare best if left outside in the fresh air. She suggested to Joseph that she return early to Israel with the boys, leaving him to finish writing his dissertation in peace. He pretended to protest but she could see he loved the idea. They packed up much of what they had acquired over the course of three years in Cambridge and took a last family outing to pick blueberries in the country before she boarded a train with the boys to catch a plane from New York.

Back in Israel, Rebecca felt elation and relief. Manfred had moved to the cottage, leaving the main house empty for her and her family, and she enjoyed every minute of every day after that. No task seemed impossible, except writing her weekly letter to Joseph. She was self-conscious about the many mistakes in her written English and the details of her life that would bore or upset him: Ethan and Noam starting to forget their English; one of the twins stuck in cow muck up to the waist, the other selecting from among marching ants, then eating them; the significant and unexplained rise in the number of eggs laid since their return to Israel; the cucumbers and tomatoes from the garden, now in a basket in the kitchen. Typewritten responses from Joseph arrived with not a single erasure or correction, and when he quoted a source, which he did often, he never failed to record its author, publisher, year of publication, and the specific pages referred to. She shared these letters with Manfred, who usually read them with a frown.

Joseph's last letter was an announcement that he had successfully defended his dissertation and would be returning to Israel in two weeks, after long months of bachelorhood. Rebecca found herself quite glad at this news. Lately she had begun to miss him in earnest and had high hopes he would return calm and optimistic, the years at Harvard behind him and a promising future teaching and writing at an Israeli university ahead. She baked a cake for the occasion and waxed the floor, and had Daniel, Ethan, and Noam draw pictures to hang on the front door in welcome. But the sullen look on his face the moment he walked in made her feel eight years old again, arriving late at a birthday party carrying the wrong gift.

"Oh, this old house," he said dispiritedly, not two minutes after returning. She, too, noticed the sagging furniture and yellowing walls, taking it all in as if for the first time. But she loved the coziness of this house, its simplicity and quiet. She knew he would want to paint the walls, reupholster the sofa, put in a lawn. "The El Al stewardesses were rude," he complained, "and the customs officers at the airport unbearable. Why is this country so poorly run?"

So she wonders why it was not relief she felt when he began spending more and more time away from home, going so often to Jerusalem for meetings with the rabbi who was helping him with the book he was writing. He kept promising to introduce them. He was sure she would love Rabbi Yoel, and wasn't it wonderful that he had found a "kindred soul"—that is what he had called him—right here in Israel? He quoted the rabbi incessantly and spoke daily with him by phone.

But she could no more have imagined those two men, her husband and this rabbi, falling in love than she could imagine tossing one of her children from a speeding car.

"We need to talk," he had said that rainy Sabbath afternoon twenty years ago, while the kids whooped and hollered in the next room. He was staring at her, standing near the kitchen sink, and continued looking into her face until she met his gaze. When he looked away she understood how serious it was. She felt a quick nervousness in her stomach. He put biscuits and two cups of chamomile tea on the table and invited her to sit with him.

What words did he use to tell her about his love for this man, about his plan to leave home that very evening, about the end of his love for her and the end of their marriage? She no longer recalls, can no longer feel the words pecking at her, though she could until just a few years ago, when she released them forever like a flock of doves. She does recall the throng of questions and images that crowded into her brain like condolence callers at a house of mourning. She sat speechless, stunned. Steam rose from her cup of tea but she could not bring herself to drink. She was doing her best to keep from retching on the kitchen table.

She watched as Joseph's sympathy for her drained away like color from a blush. He was impatient with her lack of reaction. He expected her to say something, to cry or yell, or at least ask questions. But she sat still as death. Her eyes rested on his hands, white and benign on the tabletop, and it was at this moment that the thought struck her: they were as pale and clean and work-free as the hands of the diamond merchants and the sons of the Holocaust survivors and the inbred Swiss Jews. They were foreign, these hands. They belonged elsewhere, not in her Israeli life, not on this moshav, not with her sons. "Go," she told those hands. "Leave us now."

Manfred is still at the sink, with his back to her. In these last twenty years they have never discussed Joseph's desertion. Manfred mourned his only son then went on with life. She feels a catch in her throat for this dear man, now old and lonely, his birth-year trick a thin and sorry way of trying to connect with people. She is so relieved to know he needs her, more than anyone else needs her, that she wishes she could hug

him from behind, just hold him so he will know, without her
having to utter words neither could bear, that she loves him,
not in the way her vile neighbors thought when Joseph abandoned them—she still winces when she thinks of the whispers and stares—but simply as a caring daughter should love
her dear, aging father-in-law.

How will he manage when this *batzeket* gets the best of
her? She rubs and pushes it, willing her body to swallow it
back inside itself, dissolve it, bombard it with tiny explosions
of health, anything. She is sorry now that she did not run to
the clown-haired doctor. She should have heaved this
swelling belly onto an operating table already, let them cut
out of her what her own body could not dispose of itself. She
should have had it drained, should have been tested. She
should do her best to outlive him, to nurse him to his last
breath—may he live to 120!

Perhaps, she thinks, lashing out would have stood her in
good stead. Perhaps the snake coiling itself through her
insides now would not have dared to appear had she not
given it space, had her whole being been filled up, brimming
over with fury like a pot of soup on a roaring flame. For years
she had blamed Joseph for cowardice. He had left, after all,
escaped his responsibility, run away. And she had stayed to
uphold . . . but now she recognizes another truth, one that lies
like an old cobblestone road beneath a well-traveled high-
way: perhaps it was, in fact, Joseph who was the brave one,
decisive and sure, the risk taker. He had seized an opportunity, dared to make choices, while she merely continued to
play the role he had created for her, without pause or question. And now the reunion he is holding this very weekend,
with all five of the sons he left behind, is proof of his triumph.

Life has given him love, a family, a career, and the financial resources to enjoy himself. She rubs her belly and raises her glance to her father-in-law. Are these, then, the leftovers that life has scrounged up for her: an old man, a decrepit house, a belly full of disease?

Late in the afternoon Manfred will appear with a bouquet of anemones and cyclamen he has picked from the flower garden next to his cottage. He will be neatly groomed, wearing the shirt she ironed for him this morning. His trousers will be worn to a shine but he will not allow Rebecca to buy him new ones. She will be dressed in an old gray wool skirt, too tight at the hips, and a pink blouse, with a shawl thrown over her shoulders and wrapped snugly to cover her expanding middle. Her hair will still be wet from the shower.

His only concession to age will be Rebecca's arm, upon which he will lean during their walk to the synagogue. The sun will have slid behind the dunes that block their view to the sea, and the sky will hover between light and night. High up in a eucalyptus tree, far above the remnants of the tree house the boys built and abandoned a dozen or more years ago, a family of bulbuls will chatter and squawk as it settles down for the night. Rebecca will catch a glimpse of a marten, long and low, slinking toward a neighbor's coop for a raid on the hens. He will wreak havoc there, shredding the birds to bloody pieces until he has had his fill, and will cause the death of countless others whose weak hearts will give way from fear and commotion.

Several paces past the coop Manfred will stop short. "Did you ever notice this warm current of air? Right here, always the same spot. It's only here on Shabbat, never during the week." He will tilt his head back and his nose will quiver like a dog's. "Curious," he will say, shutting his eyes. He will sway with the breeze, coming to life only when he nearly loses his balance. Rebecca will pull him forward up the path. Ahead she will see only the dome of the synagogue above the line of tall firs. She will think about what lies ahead: the peaceful service, the rabbi's short and pleasant sermon, the way the women's section glows in pale yellow light. And after services, outside the great wooden doors, how they will all stand, shivering slightly in the winter cold, how the children will play tag between their fathers' legs, how the grandparents and great-grandparents will shuffle slowly toward home, how the younger married women will parade their hats. It is almost Purim, she will think, then Passover, then Independence Day, her favorite season of the year.

All at once she will feel a deep and terrible sadness for her ex-husband. He will have missed all this; he even chose to abandon it. But she, if she can only keep sickness at bay long enough, will surely be privileged soon to watch her own grandchildren play tag here; she will witness the march of the generations and take her place in a chain of people and events that no longer has anything to do with her but in fact depends on her very existence. Her youngest son is married. Surely the older boys will begin to marry soon and then babies—a dozen at least, oh certainly more than that—will roll and tumble into her quiet life and she will make time for them all and teach them her little bits of Swiss wisdom, tell them Alpine stories, feed them European delicacies, drape a sweater over her shoulders, and push their prams around and around the moshav. Poor Joseph, she will muse. He has worked so hard to get everything he wished for, while she has wished for nothing and will be boundlessly content with the tiniest, subtlest pleasures. If only she can stay alive.

Rebecca takes several deep breaths to stem the maelstrom of tears and worry that has gathered in her chest. To her father-in-law's rounded back at the sink she says, "I just want to know what you would prefer for dessert this evening, Opa. An apple pie perhaps, or a poppy roll? Or maybe you'd prefer a chocolate ring cake." Manfred does not react at all, and Rebecca wonders whether his ears have finally reached their nineties along with the rest of him. Then, without turning around, he pronounces one word—"chocolate"—a little too loudly, and with that she knows he has been appeased and will be able to continue his morning routine. And in the very same moment, with sudden clarity, she knows precisely whom it is she must tell about the growth in her belly: Joseph, and only Joseph. She will phone him today and tell him her news. It is only right that he share the burden, and this very thought lightens her own.

"Then chocolate it shall be," she says almost cheerily to her father-in-law. She is now free to return to her own house, where two of her boys are waiting for breakfast.

* * *

"Good morning, Professor Licht!" Shlomi Buzaglo, his favorite doorman, pokes his broad and friendly face into the taxi with an offer to escort him to the entrance. Joseph enjoys the careful attentions of this cheerful young Moroccan from the working-class south side of the city. Not having noticed the drizzle that started on the way uptown, he is surprised to see Shlomi pushing a luggage cart and carrying an enormous umbrella. The umbrella is hardly necessary when all Joseph has to do is step out of the cab and walk six or seven paces to the front door, but the management of this building—the only one in Tel Aviv with two doormen round-the-clock—sets its standards by Manhattan and London, so Joseph is duly escorted.

This morning Joseph is too preoccupied for his usual reveries; he does not wonder if Rebecca has ever come to steal a peek at this lavish lobby, so different from the simple home they shared as husband and wife. He is oblivious even to the cheekiness of the second doorman, who mocks his every gesture in spite of Joseph's numerous complaints to the security manager. The young man holds the elevator doors and presses the penthouse button for him too effusively, a spurious smile pulled wide across his face.

Joseph enters the flat in a rush, tosses his keys onto an ornate secretary he and Pepe bought on auction in Budapest, and passes straight through to the cavernous kitchen. Shlomi is just rolling the luggage cart off the service elevator as Joseph opens the back door.

"Looks like you're cooking for a crowd." Shlomi's tone of voice is always amicable.

"Well, yes, I suppose I am," replies Joseph as he helps Shlomi move the bags and boxes onto the counters. He pauses to flick on the electricity and all at once the kitchen explodes in bright lights reflecting off shiny copper pans, gleaming crystal goblets, dazzling silver platters, beveled glass windowpanes, and highly polished appliances. Both men squint. "I have five sons and a daughter-in-law and they're all coming to spend the whole Shabbat with me. My boys are around your age, and they eat a lot."

Joseph takes pleasure in the look of surprise on Shlomi's face. It is the reaction he had hoped for. Shlomi could not possibly have guessed that Joseph has children, and certainly not five grown and hungry boys. "Do they visit you often?" he asks.

Joseph does not like this question and busies himself with the groceries; he shows sudden impatience with the young doorman.

But Shlomi is at heart a diplomat and looks for a way to soften matters. "We're seven brothers and sisters and my mother is always complaining we don't visit enough. So she spends all week cooking our favorites to entice us to show up on Saturday. She's not satisfied until she has at least three children and half a dozen grandkids messing up the place." As Shlomi makes space for the last bag, a large, deep purple eggplant wobbles out and thumps onto the floor.

"Oh, I'm really sorry, sir." Joseph watches the doorman pick it up and inspect it for damage, holding it close to his face and prodding it with long, thick fingers. For a shadow of a second Joseph falls back into a pocket of time when fingers like those probed his own body, young and supple then and ripe to the touch. But he quickly shakes himself free to observe Shlomi's rapt attention, so like his eldest son Daniel as a child, the way he used to lose himself in what he was doing, suddenly and completely unaware of the world around him. The bowl of a spoon, a parade of ants, a cat's-eye marble, galaxies of dust whirling in shafts of sunlight: these were Daniel's world, a shifting series of sensual diversions each more captivating than the last. "Look, it's not bruised at all," Shlomi concludes. Joseph nods and smiles; as he takes the eggplant from Shlomi he wonders how much change he has in his coin purse.

"My mother makes the best eggplant dish in the world. It's called Aubergines Rachelle, after her. King Hassan himself once invited her to make it for him at his winter palace in Marrakesh. She never gives out the recipe, but she'd probably give you a hint about the ingredients." He looks hopefully at Joseph, eager to find favor.

Joseph is anxious to be alone, itches to store the food away so he can get to work polishing the dining-room floor. "I would be happy to hear about this recipe sometime, thank you, but my menu for this weekend is set. I'm making the boys' favorites, all the dishes they liked when they were children." He stops himself, frowning at how much he has already told this young man, an employee. "Thank you for your help, Shlomi," he says, curling a twenty-shekel bill into the doorman's palm.

When Shlomi has left him, Joseph imagines the doorman's mother in a tiny flat crammed with dark-featured children helping themselves to an endless supply of unidentifiable spicy dishes and oily vegetables in small painted bowls. Sheared lamb's meat steams from a long, low platter and the fish in a tomato sauce looks just like the summer squash with gamba. The pastries are dry and flaky, then sprinkled with powdered sugar or drenched in honey. Joseph has tasted all these delicacies. Like edible perfume, they leave him feeling sticky and bloated. They are not to his liking nor, he feels certain, to his boys'.

There is no need to consult his to-do list. Joseph has looked forward to his next task all week. He wants to tire himself out on hands and knees, feel a satisfying ache climb through his upper arms, become hummingly intoxicated by the waxes and polishes. The dining-room floor was torn from a castle in Tuscany. To Joseph, caring for it is like applying creams to the skin of a peach-faced old grande dame who has been oiled, steamed, and massaged since birth and whose flesh has taken on a soft luminescence. He leans in close to inspect the grain and to marvel all the more at the floor's careful crafting, like a great seamless puzzle, how in some places it bends and swells as if defying its own strict properties. The floor was removed from the castle in one solid slab and installed still attached to the stone beneath it, so that all the other floors in the apartment needed to be raised several centimeters for parity.

But such meticulous rubbing and buffing is harder work than Joseph remembers. He feels a stiffness in his joints he knows was not there yesterday and curses himself for having left the window open through the night. The solid sheet of wood and stone beneath him does not empathize with his pains. The thick pad he has rolled out under his knees makes the effort barely bearable. He reaches the four depressions in the center of the floor, the shallow crater lakes formed by a massive dining table that sat in the same spot for two hundred years. Pepe, a fanatic for detail, had their own dining table sized to match these grooves. Joseph sits back on his heels, inspecting his work. His will to finish the job wanes as his body broadcasts, with increasing vehemence, its litany of complaints: the creak of brittle joints, the groan of chronic pain, the sigh of insulted limbs. But more than making himself sore and irritable he is afraid of finishing his chores too early and with too much listless energy intact, allowing too much time for thought and worry, so he pushes on.

He presumes Rebecca would enjoy the irony of his

circumstances, the occupant of a Tel Aviv penthouse—with hired help for the asking—down on all fours performing such a thankless task. Often, long ago, he returned home to his wife at the end of a day of studies or work, careful not to conceal his displeasure at finding the sink overflowing with dirty dishes and the laundry basket buried under mountains of dingy T-shirts and soiled socks. In the beginning Rebecca would lead him into the bathroom to show him how she had spent hours dismantling faucets to scrape loose the gathered residue, and didn't Joseph notice how the water ran in a straighter, harder stream now? Or how she had patched the boys' frayed trouser knees or tinkered with the fridge to stop its incessant clanging or swept the chicken coop or bathed the dog. Still, he couldn't bring himself to see beyond the dishes and the laundry, and eventually Rebecca hardened: she stopped making her reports and left the sink and hamper fuller than before. Now, despite the demands of a fairly successful academic career, Joseph's real vocation is that of *hausfrau*, a position he only mildly resents. He wants this rich, ancient wood to glow in small pools of yellow light, wishes to capture the reflected sparkle of crystal in its polished surface.

Growing up at Sde Hirsch he was certainly the only boy who could cook and sew, not because he particularly enjoyed those occupations but because teaching him was his mother's way of spending time with him while tending to the endless needs of a demanding husband. Manfred never explained what he wanted; he simply left her a list of chores and errands each morning on the kitchen table. These lists—written in German despite his complete ban on speaking that language—formed the center of her world, his likes and dislikes the pillar of smoke that guided them by day and the pillar of fire that guided them by night. So Joseph learned the proper way to iron a shirt (arms first, collar, sides, back), how to squeeze, poke, and shake fresh produce, when to stop whipping cream, how to mop the floors of an entire house using one small bucket of water. He can soft-boil an egg to perfection, and when he relieves a pomelo of its peel it becomes a flower exploding into bloom. He knows dozens of recipes by heart and can wash a ritual prayer shawl without entangling a single strand of *tzitzit* fringe with its neighbor. He can turn any overripe fruit into compote and has five or six tricks for saving stale bread from the waste bin.

Joseph finishes with the floor and after edging the massive table, in tiny increments, back into its grooves, stands facing the room from the slate tiles in the kitchen. Even in the plain gray light of this day its beauty is palpable. He would like to put his cheek to it as a sculptor might embrace the creation at which he has so lovingly hacked and chiseled.

Five recipes are lined up on the kitchen counter. Joseph shuffles their various requirements into one complex plan of action. In place of lunch he tops some thin rye and onion crackers with camembert and avocado, and these he eats standing over the sink, careful not to sprinkle crumbs on the polished countertop. Twelve egg whites for the angel food cake need to breathe and expand for one hour before being beaten. The filo pastry Joseph removed from the freezer last night has completely thawed, but before embarking on the broccoli strudel he detours to the mushroom moussaka, slicing and salting the eggplant and laying out the purple-edged ovals in an oblong colander perched over the sink, to sweat out the bitter juices. He slides the vegetable steamer from its compartment, measuring and pouring water and rice—which for Gideon's meticulous religious observance he scrutinizes for impurities like tiny pebbles or insects—and thinks briefly of Rebecca as he pours the dozen useless angel food yolks down the drain. She always disapproved of the Birthday Cake, which Joseph suspected was due to the waste involved. She would rescue the yolks, intending to find some way to use them, but invariably they would sit in the refrigerator, sometimes for weeks, until one of the boys tipped the bowl over or Joseph surreptitiously disposed of them.

For the chocolate mousse Joseph separates five more eggs, but these yolks he places in a small bowl and that into a larger bowl containing hot water. The smallest electric hand mixer is ideal for the required twenty minutes of very gradual beating. Joseph begins to feel the veins in his calves swelling up and after a minute of beating he moves the whole operation from the island in the middle of the kitchen to the counter at the window, where he can sit on a stool and watch the boats in the marina bob on the waves.

All the thoughts and images in Joseph's mind pop like flimsy bubbles of soap the moment the phone rings. He is so startled that he forgets even to worry about it being one of the boys phoning to cancel.

"Hello, Joseph," she says carefully.

His ex-wife has not called in years, and though her voice is frayed and full of fatigue, he recognizes it at once. "Rebecca, nice to hear from you. How are you?"

She considers for a moment. The question and the potential answer are far more loaded than Joseph could imagine, but she is not going to tell him everything just now. Not yet. She wants to discuss another matter first. "It's your father," she says at last.

Joseph holds his breath. Manfred turned ninety this year, but Joseph has not seen him, heard from him, or spoken with him in twenty years. A most ungracious thought crosses his mind: he hopes his aging father will not ruin his birthday and reunion weekend by dying just now.

"He has been behaving strangely lately, and yesterday afternoon he had some sort of attack. We got him to the hospital in Hadera, but even though he's come back home for Shabbat I know he is not doing well. I think maybe you should visit him."

"Rebecca, you know I have no problem visiting him. He's the one who wants no contact with me. Why would you think that's changed? Has he said anything?"

"Of course not. But still . . . the time has come for you to take over. Whether he is willing or not. I'm not able . . . I cannot . . ." She falters, her resolve dissipating. The words she needs to describe her malady have clogged in her mouth, made her tongue their prisoner. Once, early in their marriage, his ability to see what was in her thoughts had seemed uncanny to her, but time and distance have made them near strangers. She can hear the impatience in his breathing. The moment has passed and she is both sorry and relieved.

"Joseph," she says, her heart settling back to its normal rate, "we need to talk. I have a problem and I will . . . need your help. But I'll let you get through your Sabbath with the boys first. How about coffee in town next week?"

"Fine, fine."

"Fine," she repeats. Just as she is poised to return the receiver to the cradle she remembers something. "Joseph, did Noam phone you?"

He stiffens. "No, I haven't heard from him."

"Hmmmm. I was afraid of that. He told me he couldn't get a flight before Shabbat, but he promised he would call you."

"A flight? Where is he?"

"Spain somewhere. Modeling for a television commercial. I thought you knew."

Joseph gazes out at the empty sea. He says nothing.

"Well," Rebecca says kindly, "perhaps this means he'll manage to arrive on time."

"Perhaps," Joseph echoes weakly before they hang up.

Joseph feels cold and hollow. His father is ill; his middle son, the easiest one, is missing and may not be on hand for the celebration; Rebecca has something to discuss with him after so many years of silence. Overwhelmed and fatigued, Joseph is tempted to crawl into bed, but instead he wills himself to turn his full attention to the egg whites for the angel food cake, which have been breathing for just over an hour. He is pensive as he watches their transformation from clear, gluey liquid to the frothing peaks that remind him of Switzerland, the nation that gave him both a mother and a wife. He thinks this cake must turn out as white and pristine as those iced mountains, the way Daniel and all the boys loved it. And then everything will be fine.

* * *

When the wind kicks up, teasing the daughters' skirts skyward but leaving the mother's synthetic wig unruffled, Gavriel glances at his watch. In fact, he knows what time it is. This strange, low wind blows every day just after noon, more accurate than any clock. Nothing surprises him here anymore. He thinks of these rock-strewn hills as bewitched and bewitching and his love for them is physical. Most of the winter rains have fallen and the hills have taken on a lush softness, carpets of bright green grass covering them like moss. He dreams often of cupping these hills in giant hands, caressing them like breasts. He imagines himself rolling naked from hill to valley and up hill again, then chides himself for such sensuality.

The early *minha* prayer services will begin in less than an hour and he still has quite a bit to cover with this family of Orthodox American Jews, but they have asked too many irrelevant and misguided questions for which he invariably provides long answers, so he has fallen far behind schedule and worries he may miss the last bus to Tel Aviv before the Sabbath. Of all his brothers he has been most vociferous about taking part in their father's celebration. How could he, of any of them, fail to show up?

"It is generally believed," he says, pointing to the valley beneath them, "that this is the route the Patriarch Abraham took from his home in Beersheva to Mount Moriah, where he went to sacrifice his son Isaac. And Jacob would have used this same route when he left his father-in-law's house and returned to the homeland from which he'd run away, now with his wives and—who knows how many sons?"

The middle daughter, plump and giggly, shouts, "Twelve!" Gavriel looks to the parents and the other children for confirmation. The eldest daughter puckers her lips and blows him a secret kiss from behind her father's back. She has been licking her lips or fondling herself or winking or making some other lewd gesture all afternoon. Each time, she catches his attention but not that of her parents or sisters and by now Gavriel is almost accustomed to it. He hopes to take the father aside before they part to warn him of his daughter's highly unsuitable behavior.

"Ah, but not yet," he corrects. The middle daughter's smile droops while the eldest daughter hugs herself suggestively. "The Matriarch Rachel is about to give birth to number twelve, little Benjamin, but only when the family reaches Efrat, just up the road." The father, obese and unshaven, nods knowingly. The mother pats the middle daughter's shoulder in consolation.

This family is slower than most, Gavriel thinks. They look properly religious—the father's *tzitzit* fringes dangle freely from his waist to his knees; the girls' skirts reach the bottom of their shoes, sweeping and collecting the dirt of the Holy Land—but they are not taking a real interest in his stories the way most of his tourists do. And the eldest daughter! There is clearly something not quite right in this household. He checks his watch again. There will be no time to visit the site of the battle between David and Goliath. They will have to head straight north to Rachel's Tomb if they want to finish before *minha*. Anyway, he has accomplished the most important part of the tour, showing them the settlement he helped found: Har Baruch, not so surreptitiously named for the man who gunned down fifty-two Muslims in prayer exactly two years ago this month. Temporarily comprising several caravans and a few tin shacks on a wind-blasted slope in a lonely corner of the hills south of Hebron, Har Baruch has become the home of a few sturdy individuals—five bachelors and two newly married couples—devoted to a life of austerity and commitment to reclaiming every inch of Judea and Samaria from Arabs. They raise sheep, grow many

slowly in the sun. Gavriel finds these moments intensely painful. He wonders if the smile on Shilo's face comes from thoughts of their friend's wife back at the settlement. He thinks Shilo seeks out a prostitute in Tel Aviv now and again, but he cannot be sure about this.

Har Baruch has become a whole world for Gavriel. He has been sucked into the tiniest nuances of the place. He notices everything, but most especially the people, all eight of them. He knows all their idiosyncrasies, their quirks, their tics. He feels he could write books about each of them, and indeed he takes notes in an alphabet only he can read, but he will never betray what he has learned about them. He knows already that he will have to leave this place, even leave Shilo, but he is not ready and is almost hopeful that something large and dramatic and fateful will take place. However, he will never willingly be the catalyst.

Gavriel is too busy to return home to the moshav——that part of Israel seems like a different country to him—but he tries to speak with his mother once a week. He rarely contacts his father and has never asked him for anything. He maintains good relations with his brothers, but mostly they refuse to visit him at Har Baruch, which upsets him.

Rachel's Tomb is swarming with busloads of Israeli tourists, mostly older women in mismatched clothing and head scarves. To Gavriel it looks like a convention of cleaning ladies. His American tourists have tired of his wordy explanations; they have gone missing in the tangle of biblical verses he's quoted and are confused by modern Israeli politics, so many Shimons and Yitzhaks and Haims who have signed this or that accord. They are more interested in tying thin red strings to their wrists like all the women who have come to

Rachel's Tomb in hopes of blessings: good health, sturdy and sober husbands for their daughters, honest jobs for their sons. Gavriel sputters, his prolixity cut to shreds by constant interruptions. Soon only the father is paying attention to him at all. Even the eldest daughter has given up on him and is flirting with the soldiers guarding the tomb's entrance.

Gavriel heads Har Baruch's attack-proof vehicle back toward the town of Efrat, where the family's car is parked and where they will find a minyan for afternoon prayers. While the women stop for coffee and a pastry, Gavriel and the father walk up the hill toward the synagogue.

"You have a very nice family," Gavriel begins diplomatically, in search of a gentle way to broach this difficult subject. "But I must tell you that your eldest daughter has been making inappropriate advances toward me all afternoon." He holds his breath after the last word, convinced he is right for having mentioned her but jittery nonetheless.

It is only two uphill blocks from the coffee shop to the synagogue, but the overweight father stops, winded. "You think I don't notice what she's up to? It makes me sick! At least here in Israel she picks on Jews mostly, except for the Arab waiters." He jabs Gavriel hard in the forearm. He is shouting now, and Gavriel is relieved that no one else is on the street at the moment. "The bitch needs a man, fast!" the father bellows. "I'd marry her off tomorrow if I could. Big wedding, I'll set you up in business, put you in a nice clean house in Brooklyn." He is nearly purple with exertion and anger, the stubble standing out from his face. Then he checks his rage. "She flirts," he winks, "but she's still a virgin."

Gavriel is shocked into silence. He stares open mouthed at this coarse and corpulent American. The man pulls his arm. "Come on; we'll be late for *minha*." He continues up the hill. "Cool off, I didn't think you'd bite but I had to try, didn't I? Father's obligation. *May the good lord free me from this punishment!*" he recites in Hebrew, paraphrasing a prayer. "You impress me as a real innocent and you're probably looking for a quiet little girl. You won't marry for money either, will you? I'm a pretty good judge of character, and I've got you pegged for an idealist. Right? How else could you live in that pigsty you took us to? Why else would you turn your nose up at a perfectly good marriage proposal, with a job and a house for a dowry?"

They have reached the synagogue and the American puffs his way through the door ahead of Gavriel and sits in a corner, clearly signaling his desire to be left alone. Gavriel spots Shilo in an instant. He has been selected to lead the prayers and is making his way forward to the pulpit. Gavriel threads his way through the small crowd to the front, where few people have taken seats, and stands just feet away from Shilo.

Happy are those who dwell in your house. They will sing your praises. The congregation comes to attention, echoing Shilo's call to prayers. Gavriel recites the psalm, enunciating and pondering each holy word He closes his eyes and sways. *Open your hand*, he intones with intensity, *and satisfy the desire of all creatures.* Shilo has reached the Half-Kaddish, which will launch them into the silent benedictions. Gavriel breathes in Shilo's voice as if it were smoke. It spreads through his body, dense and husky. His eyes still closed, he pictures Shilo swaying, the slow forward thrust of his hips. He squeezes his eyes shut tighter and tilts his chin toward heaven. *Forgive us our sins. . . . Look down upon our misery. . . .*

*We are guilty. . . . We have lusted. . . . You know our evil inclina-
tions, remember that we are merely dust. . . . Save us and forgive
our sins for your sake.*

When Gavriel opens his eyes he sees Shilo leaning over a
podium, engrossed in a book. The prayers have ended and
only a few men remain in the synagogue. He is surprised he
has managed to lose himself in prayer, escaping the torture of
his obsession so completely. As a fatherless boy Gavriel spent
years choosing fathers from among the men of the moshav.
He would decide that one man or another was really his
father—Joseph, in his rare appearances, seemed more like a
distant, dignified city uncle—and he would devise ways to
spend time with him. He learned to milk cows when he chose
Shimon Altman during the summer holidays when he was
almost nine, and he spent every afternoon for one whole winter
in the metalworking shop of Avi Epelbaum. He was especially happy when they tousled his hair or winked and whispered that their own sons weren't half the help he was.
Gavriel learned to be more circumspect after his grandfather
upbraided him for jumping onto Mordechai Zeeman's lap
during a Torah study group, but he loved nothing better than
inhaling the smells and touching the rough clothes and work-
worn bodies of these rugged moshav men. He knows now to
bury his passion under layers of indifference, but the crafty
smile Shilo is flashing his way disarms him. Not for the first
time he fears that Shilo knows exactly what is on his mind.

Shilo puts down his book. "Your brother Ethan called. He
wants to know what time you'll be arriving at your father's
this evening." He is still grinning with mischief.

Gavriel hangs his head, caught in a lie. He told Shilo and
all the others he would be at his mother's for Shabbat, hoping

to avoid their harangues: "He's loaded, your father. Why can't you get him to make a donation?" "Let Shilo pay him a visit; then we'll see some money." "Tell your father this is the real Israel, not Tel Aviv." They do not let him forget Joseph's one visit to Har Baruch, how one of his black leather Bally boots had sunk in the deep mud, how he kept smoothing down his hair, blown out of place by the strong winds. They would probably leave the topic alone if they knew about his father's relationship with Pepe, would treat Gavriel as an orphan, but the silent recriminations would be more than he could bear so he has told no one, not even Shilo.

"All right, pal, I'll let you off the hook. I won't hassle you this time and I won't even tell the others. But next time don't lie to me. We're too close for that bullshit."

Gavriel's gratitude and relief win out over his skepticism. He feels himself filling up, flooding with something. He thinks it is love, but he cannot know for sure. He beams at Shilo, shines his inner light at him, feels his heart jump toward him, but Shilo is buried in his book, and Gavriel's love and light and energy, once again, have nowhere to go.

* * *

The cake is on the cooling rack, the casseroles in the oven, and the mousse has settled in to its place in the refrigerator. The Jaffa port is suddenly ablaze in a spotlight of sun, odd for late winter but comforting to Joseph in his large, quiet flat. The houses at Sde Hirsch crouch to the earth every one, shunning skyward aspirations—second stories, chimneys, peaked roofs—paying homage instead to the dirt that provides their occupants' living, the soil of Eretz Israel that sustains their souls, too. Since leaving the moshav, Joseph has always chosen to live on the top floor of every building, including a sixth-floor walk-up, in order to be as high above the settled dust, crawling insects, and squabbling humans as possible. At fifty he is no longer bitter about the simple folks of Sde Hirsch. They work hard, live frugally, and offer prayers to God with astonishing regularity. He no longer agonizes about their mindless devotion, and in weak moments wonders if that isn't what God intended for mortals all along.

Joseph has not yet decided about attending services this weekend with his sons. He is nurturing a hope they will ask him to accompany them to the synagogue even though he cannot imagine himself singing the old Sabbath tunes or rocking back and forth in an ecstasy of prayer. Those are part of his buried life. Instead, he thinks he may just sit alone in the Sabbath Eve quiet, enjoying the purr of the kitchen and the thought of the pleasant weekend ahead of him, waiting for his sons to return.

He moves on to the heavier foods and before long the kitchen fills with the smell of cooking meat. The soup is boiling, the chicken is in the oven, and the beef is roasting slowly over an open grill. These slippery slabs of flesh, these pieces of anatomy from dumb and dirty animals, nearly caused Joseph to retch as he cleaned and seasoned them. Now they prick his nostrils and tease his tongue and he knows he will have to sample them until he's had his fill.

Unlike the slovenly beef and chicken, the fish puts up a fight. Its innards are nearly impossible to remove and Joseph wages war with a knife. The fish was a gamble from the beginning and now he is not certain if it is worth it. He has substituted several ingredients and is not even sure his sons will eat fish, especially one cooked with peanuts and coconut.

Maybe this Brazilian recipe—a tangible connection to Pepe—
is a mistake. Perhaps Joseph should have shut him out completely. At the very moment Joseph gives up on the fish its
inner organs come free and in a second they are washed
away down the drain.

It is past midday, and Joseph's morning aches are joined
by a stiff neck and sore legs. He picks up the phone and
punches in a low number on the speed dial.

Philippe answers on the first ring.

"I'm in pain. Can you come over?"

Joseph resents the slight pause. Philippe is never forthcoming over the phone. "It is essential?"

"*Absolument*," says Joseph, hopeful.

Philippe sighs. "*J'arrive*," he says, and hangs up.

Joseph takes a bar of scouring soap from under the
kitchen sink and steps into the glass-doored shower next to
his bedroom. He acknowledges the difficult morning he has
had by the odors and tints he scrubs from his sore limbs. He
wraps himself in a thick cotton robe and steps through to the
small adjacent exercise room. After spreading a sheet across
the massage table and rolling a small table next to it he dims
the lights, then heads for the pantry to fetch Philippe a bottle
of sparkling water.

Joseph knows Philippe's reluctance is due more to ego than
time and that it will still be a while before he arrives. So he
decides to indulge himself: he squats before the glass-topped
table of photographs in the living room but does not study any
particular snapshot, reaching instead into a tiny secret drawer
underneath. He removes an envelope, rises with difficulty, and
lets himself fall backward gently onto an overstuffed divan.

With great care and a touch of reverence he slides the

brittle sheets of onionskin paper from the envelope. One page
has separated into two along a crease. He greets the familiar
handwriting—crimped, strained, private, so unlike the huge-
ness of Yoel's body and personality—with the relief of finding a loved one restored in good health after a long journey
and nods in recognition to twenty years of spots and stains.
He does not lift the pages to his face. He knows they possess
no scent of their owner. They smell only of time.

Dearest Love,

*I am saturated with the love of our last meeting, as though
the bones and blood and tissue have been removed from my
body and replaced with pure light, a holy radiance suffused
with the breath of angels.*

Joseph gazes up, away from the letter, at nothing. He
sinks into the moist lushness, ready as always to abandon all
sense and logic for the passion he only dimly recalls, a bright
green jungle visited too many years ago. He recites out loud,
from memory, what he has just read and imagines a flight—
his own—from the mortal to the immortal, from the corpore-
al to the ethereal, a straight shot skyward from earth to the
airy light of a rainbow.

*I feel it swirling inside me, frothing; it makes me light and
buoyant, I am a bubble on a wave, a butterfly on a breeze. I
see only stars and moonlight, hear only symphonies. I cannot
work, I have no need for sleep, no desire for food, but when I
do read or taste or dream it is always you that my ears or
tongue or heart wishes to recapture. I have sought out G-d
my whole life*

The buzzer sounds. Joseph stops reading but remains motionless for a moment. He feels flattened and small, folded into the deep couch. When the buzzer sounds again he remembers to breathe and rises slowly, carefully sliding the pages into the envelope and that into his robe pocket.

Philippe does not stop in greeting at the front door, but proceeds straight to the exercise room, calling out a reminder to Joseph to bring his water in a tall, fluted glass. It is Philippe's cologne that brings Joseph back to his senses. So this is what the young men are wearing today, he thinks as he follows Philippe and the scent. He knows this is how they sniff each other out, these sculpted men in thin, tight clothes and stylish haircuts. He knows they have their signs and codes, every gesture and trinket and label signaling to like-minded boys who they are and what they want. To Joseph the code is like trying to read hieroglyphs: the intricacy of their symbols fascinates him but ultimately leaves him on the outside, bewildered.

Philippe is already unpacking his bag when Joseph catches up with him. As he removes ten or twelve tiny vials from a leather case he tells Joseph, in his typical mixture of French and English, that aromatherapy is what he needs today.

Joseph waits to be told to remove his bathrobe, part of the routine. "*Vas-y, mon cher,*" says Philippe impatiently. "I haven't got all day."

He considers telling Philippe to leave. The stiffness in his neck has subsided and he wishes to check the young masseur's impertinence. Instead he turns his back to Philippe and tosses the robe onto an exercise bike. He does not dare look at himself naked. He knows his flat stomach has given way to a small pout of a belly, a middle thickened by age and good living. His sole and paltry consolation is that Philippe, too, will one day face the same fate. Without turning toward the young man he climbs onto the table and lies on his stomach.

"Tell Philippe where it hurts, *chéri.*" Joseph is glad that his tone has softened and he relaxes as Philippe covers his lower half with a white sheet.

"Shoulders. Neck. Lower back. Behind the knees. Feet." Joseph pictures himself on all fours, polishing the dining-room floor. "I've been working hard around here. My sons and my daughter-in-law are coming to visit for the Sabbath."

Philippe is applying oils to Joseph's shoulders and neck. The warmth spreads downward as Philippe's fingers prod and pull. "A full house. So why you don't have more help? Certainly Monsieur Pepe can pay for it!"

Joseph shrugs off the question. Philippe invariably mentions Pepe's money and Joseph knows he cannot make the young Frenchman understand how important it is for him to perform these tasks himself, that his reunion will not be earned if not by sweat and suffering.

Philippe launches into a story about a client of his, a lawyer he services in his office. The gentle massage and warm oils lull Joseph and set him adrift from the masseur's tale. His sore muscles are softening, his resistance thawing. He thinks of Yoel, who knew less than Philippe about giving a massage but whose touch held love, and Joseph could always feel this. His hands first caught Joseph's attention that day in the Yeshurun Synagogue of Jerusalem more than twenty years ago. Huge hands they were, swollen and strong, but supple and soft to the touch. Those hands told Joseph, all the way from up on the stage, before he ever touched them, that there was something about Rabbi Yoel that did not add up. What use had a Torah scholar for the hands of a craftsman?

Joseph's pelvis tilts in to the table as Philippe presses hard on his lower back. "So I tell him a low leather couch will never do and you know what he does? He pushes all his important papers onto the floor as if they are old newspapers and lies down right on his desk with his legs hanging off the end and his feet on top of a shelf of books. So I know this man has a great need for me." Philippe's stories always contain an element of his contribution to humanity, but while Joseph grimaces into the pillow, his interest has been kindled and he waits for more.

"I think when I see him he is *moche*, you know, really ugly. But I turn him over and I get a big, wonderful surprise. He is North African; I think this has something to do with it. A rich, successful lawyer and *énorme, quelle joie!* Since then I go every week, sometimes twice." Philippe has pulled back the sheet, his fingers prodding and poking too urgently. Joseph is about to remind Philippe not to touch him there when Philippe turns him over and grabs hold of his stiffening penis. "So lovely," says Philippe, but Joseph suspects he is thinking about his dark and homely lawyer.

Joseph tries to abandon himself to the pleasure of Philippe's hand but instead he worries. Was it really sore shoulders that forced him to call for help, or this, the paid services of a French goy in Israel on forged papers provided by an Arab lover? Pepe would want to hear the details, but there would be nothing to tell. A dirty story, flesh rubbing flesh. The same everywhere, forever.

It did not begin this way, Joseph reminds himself. Back then it was entirely different, that rich passion he had known once, the absolute ecstasy of loving one human being who loved him in return with the same measure of excitement and pleasure and desire and respect. From the time they met, Joseph knew Yoel Rosenzweig was the one, the love against whom all others would be compared.

"It is said that since completing the creation of the universe, God has occupied himself with matchmaking." Yoel told Joseph this once as they lay sprawled on a blanket in a quiet corner of the botanical gardens early on in their relationship, as their friendship blossomed and their romance waxed.

Joseph had misunderstood. "So that explains how we found one another," he said with a broad grin.

"Ah, but no, my love, I was referring to this flower. *Ophrys apifera*. A member of the orchid family. Look, a whole patch of them growing here." His massive hands cupped and separated one flower from the rest with a tenderness that aroused Joseph. "What does its shape remind you of?"

"A bee, I suppose," Joseph said with indifference.

"Exactly! That is precisely what the male bee thinks, too, as he tries to mate with it. To him this flower even *smells* and *feels* like a female bee and that's why he pollinates it."

"Silly fool!"

"Listen to what it says here: 'The flower emits a substance that behaves like the bees' sex hormone. Each type of *Ophrys apifera* attracts only one type of male bee, each of which pollinates in a manner unique to this species, called pseudocopulation.'"

"Sounds awful!"

"Quiet, please. 'The male bee first locates the flower by smell, then as he approaches he identifies it by sight, and finally by feel. After landing on the flower the bee rubs itself over the surface in a back-and-forth motion that simulates copulation and the pollen sticks to his head before he realizes he has been misled and flies to another flower . . .'"

"Not having learned his lesson, the stupid bee . . ."

" . . . where of course he completes the act of pollination."

"Bravo. But what does all that have to do with divine matchmaking?" Joseph's interest was at last fully engaged.

"Only God could bring these two creatures together in such perfect symbiotic harmony."

Joseph raised himself onto one elbow. "Do you really believe that? I mean, what about millions, *billions* of years of evolution? You're simply too intelligent to hide behind biblical ignorance in the face of what we know of the universe today."

Yoel left the flower and turned to Joseph. "I do believe you're changing on me. You seem less and less inclined to look to the Torah for answers and more likely to trust Western science and literature alone."

"Well . . ."

"Let me tell you something, Joseph," Yoel said as he shifted to a sitting position. "Whatever you do, wherever your mind takes you, don't forsake your heritage. It has more riches to offer than you could ever imagine. And you'll see, if you look long and hard enough, and with a loving eye, you can reconcile virtually everything."

"Everything?" Joseph asked suspiciously.

"I believe so. I've personally tackled some of the toughest

issues—slaughter and annihilation in the Torah and the racism that stems from being the Chosen People, to name two—and resolved or rationalized or explained them for myself. I've written articles to share my ideas with others. It's an ongoing process, and it gives me faith and courage."

Joseph sat up and faced Yoel. "And what about us?" he asked.

"Us?"

"Yes, us. How do you explain and rationalize our relationship?"

Yoel looked up into the trees at a raven cawing shrilly. He met Joseph's gaze but did not smile. "It seems to me that Moses provided us with the shape, the essence of Judaism. He showed us that there are two paths, that of Jewish law, which provides us with order and continuity and meaning."

"And?"

Yoel snapped a thick branch in half. "And the path of hedonism and self-interest, a life without constraints."

Joseph shook his head slowly in disbelief. "You mean to tell me that you think our relationship is hedonistic? That all we're out for is pleasure?" His voice contained no small measure of hurt. "What about the genuine love and camaraderie we feel for one another?"

"Joseph, nobody but us gains anything at all from our . . . friendship, and many, including us, stand to be hurt by it. If that isn't self-interest and hedonism then I don't know what is."

Joseph had never before felt anything but contentment and love in Yoel's company, but now his anger was flaring. "To quote from your precious Talmud, the ideal student-teacher relationship is one in which the pupil 'eats with him, drinks with him, and sleeps with him, to reveal all his secrets.' Isn't that the two of us? The sages would have blessed us!"

"Oh, Joseph, what a distortion. Of course that's not what they meant!"

The two men had reached an impasse, a conflict in a relationship each had secretly, impossibly hoped would live forever in unblemished harmony. They fell silent for a moment, and gazed at anything but one another.

Yoel addressed the breach first. "In any event," he said slowly, "we have not transgressed the commandment 'And you shall not lie with a man as a woman.'"

"How not? Why just an hour ago . . ."

"No." Yoel shook his head firmly. "Jewish law is quite clear on this point. There is only one explicitly forbidden act." He looked hopefully to Joseph for signs of comprehension.

"Only one?" Joseph asked timidly.

"Only one," Yoel answered gravely. "On all the rest the sages are silent. So we have not transgressed God's law."

Joseph contemplated this news silently for several minutes while Yoel returned to the bee flowers.

"And what is the punishment if we *do* transgress?"

"Don't ask," Yoel said quietly without turning around.

"Voilà, c'est fini," says Philippe, as if to a child. Joseph understands only when the masseur has released his grip. Is this another trick of Philippe's profession or an additional humiliation of encroaching old age? How had he not felt it coming? It is only as Philippe peels them back and tosses them into a bin that Joseph notices the soiled rubber gloves he must have surreptitiously slipped over his hands.

*

Joseph awakens in the darkened, windowless exercise room unsure where he is. His only indication is the dim boiler light on the hot tub. Usually a light sleeper, he wonders how Philippe could have covered him with a comforter from the bedroom and left the flat without waking him. Briefly he wrestles with the possibility that Philippe somehow drugged him and escaped with suitcases stuffed with silver and paintings. He remembers the food in the oven and bolts for the kitchen. There he finds the fish, chicken, and beef lined up in a row on the counter, as if poised at the start of a race. Joseph is too embarrassed by his own suspicions to call Philippe to thank him, but he makes a mental note to buy him a very good bottle of wine.

*   *   *

On Fridays Gideon stays for the late-morning *shiur*, the last lesson of the day before the students disperse in order to prepare for the Sabbath. But on this particular Friday it is hard for him to concentrate on the rabbi's words, so he pinches himself every so often in an attempt to put his mind on track again. The pinches do not help, however. His father's image appears and reappears in his mind. Sometimes Joseph is wearing a bright red dress with ruffles at the bottom and sometimes a white and frilly wedding gown and sometimes a long black fur coat. His hair is dyed white blond and his fingernails seem to be painted.

The more Gideon imagines his father, the more distraught he becomes. Joseph has promised he will prepare and serve the food on newly toiveled cookware. He says he has bought only the most kosher of foods. But Gideon cannot bear the thought of being in that house of sin, as if he condones his father's aberrant lifestyle. And what if that other man is there—how can he and Batya possibly be part of a desecration of the holy Sabbath? To where will they escape if necessary? They know no one in Tel Aviv.

His apprehension runs deeper than that, however. Gidi was never popular with the older boys. He was critical of them and he complained a lot as a child, commanding more than his fair share of their mother's attention. He was the best and most intense student of the five of them, and it was no secret that Rebecca and especially Manfred derived immense pleasure from his successes in school. At Sabbath meals Manfred would often quiz his grandsons on their knowledge of the Bible and it was usually only Gideon who could answer all his questions. He is in no mood to be made fun of by his brothers, and he knows that Batya is no match for their wit. He prefers to stay at home, with people just like him. The thought that his whole family is estranged from him makes him abysmally sad.

Gideon pulls his fur hat far down over his ears before he sets out toward home in the cold air. He is pleased to find that their home—two rooms that jut into the courtyard of Batya's parents' apartment—is warm today. He is grateful for this arrangement, which enables them to remain in their densely crowded and terribly expensive ultra-Orthodox Jerusalem neighborhood of Mea She'arim. He finds Batya in their bedroom when he arrives.

She smiles and hugs herself when she sees him. "I prayed to God you would walk in right now, and you did!" Her face breaks into a wide and glowing smile.

The simplicity of her belief always rankles Gideon. "Don't you know that's ridiculous? Batya, don't you know how stupid that sounds?" He watches the smile melt from her face. "You can't say things like that at my father's house."

"Gideon, why not?" Her face is as innocent as a toddler's.

"My father is a very clever man. You don't want him to think you're stupid, do you? Just behave yourself, with him and with my brothers, and maybe we'll get through this."

"Get through what?"

"This awful weekend!" He is shouting now.

"Gideon?"

"What?"

"Will you help me decide what clothes to bring along?"

Several months before Gideon's twenty-first birthday, the head of his yeshiva assembled all the men who studied there—the married ones, the army-age group, the high school students—along with all the teachers, in order to announce that a star pupil, Gideon Licht, would marry his daughter Batya. There was ecstatic rejoicing at the yeshiva for two days. The announcement was met with somewhat less enthusiasm at home in Sde Hirsch, but within the week invitations were sent out. The wedding took place in a large hall adjacent to the yeshiva, with one thousand guests in attendance. In protest Rebecca had refused to buy a new dress for this first wedding of a son, but she did eventually purchase a hat and shoes for the occasion. Noam led the entire family to believe he would not attend, but he showed up—with a young lady none of them had met before, the straps of her cocktail dress constantly slipping off shoulders only partially hidden by a carelessly wrapped shawl—just as the ceremony was getting under way. Noam and his date left before the meal when they realized that men and women were required to eat on opposite sides of a partition, separated for the entire affair. Joseph, the father of the groom, was not invited, nor was his name mentioned on the invitation.

Gideon is a moody husband, though charming to Batya's parents, siblings, and virtually everyone else. Still, in such close quarters it is hard to hide anything, and they know his patience is tried constantly. They do not blame him. Batya has not been right since a family holiday at an ultra-Orthodox hotel at the seashore during her eighth summer. A nameless, faceless man pulled her into a room by her braids as she walked down the hotel corridor, perhaps the only time she had ever been free of all of her seven siblings—her parents had divided the children for the day and each thought Batya was with the other—and performed unspeakable acts on her for hours and hours. He threatened her at knifepoint never to say a word to anyone and made tiny incisions in her thighs to make sure she understood. Batya did not speak a word for more than four years, her child's mind certain her attacker had meant never to say *any* word to *any*one, until her menstrual bleeding began and her need to ask questions strangled her fears.

Gideon for the most part suppresses his physical urges under layers of heavy clothing. On occasion, more often than not on a Friday evening, he gives in and takes Batya to bed. She is pliant, if not particularly enthusiastic, but she understands she will not conceive a child if she does not lie with her husband. And a baby of her own is the thing she wants most in the world, along with making Gideon happy. They do not know why they have not conceived after more than a year of marriage, but they have done no tests to find out. Batya has asked her mother about this, but the woman tells her God will provide, so Batya is waiting patiently for him to provide, and she continues to respond to her husband's urges with this in mind. Batya would be surprised to know she is not the only person to wonder whether that bad man from the hotel at the seashore took all the babies out of her, but this is a question she never asks.

*   *   *

Relieved and still relaxed from the massage and the nap, Joseph wanders drowsy and dreamy into the center of the living room, assessing it in a slow twirl. He has already banished Géricault's nude laborer to his bedroom wall. From the coffee table he removes *DanceErotica* and *The Male Nude in Sculpture*, but leaves *The Opera Sets of David Hockney* after flipping through to be sure. He places Pepe's collection of teakwood primitives in a lined wicker basket and covers it with a cloth, brushing his hand lightly over the bulbous breasts and pointy phalluses now jutting upward from a bed of satin. He has always found these crude and cheap and plans to keep them hidden even after the weekend, until Pepe registers their disappearance. He suddenly notices two whole shelves of books—novels, short story collections, poetry anthologies, essays—that could cause problems. He does not want to haul them all away, and to where? He wishes he could cover them with a sheet, like the supermarkets do with the leavened food during Passover week, but then decides to leave them all. *This* is my life, he reminds himself.

Joseph jumps as the intercom buzzes. "The beverage shop has delivered your order," says Shlomi Buzaglo, the doorman. "Is it OK if I bring it up now?"

When he arrives at the kitchen door Joseph is surprised

to find Shlomi looking slightly disheveled. He is capless, and the two top buttons of his uniform are open, spilling curly black hair out of the opening. "I'm off duty now," he tells Joseph, sensitive to his stare. "Last little chore before I go." Shlomi wheels a luggage cart with three cartons of beer and wine and soft drinks and juices directly to the pantry. "Shall I unpack any of these straight into the fridge?" he asks in a strained voice as he bends over the heavy boxes.

"No, no. I'll do that later."

"Sure smells great in here." He approaches Joseph in the middle of the kitchen. "You certainly didn't need my mom's recipe," he adds amicably.

Joseph knows the pockets of his bathrobe are empty, but he slides his hands down the sides of his legs anyway, hoping an unplanned coin will materialize from nowhere.

"Oh, please, no tips today. If anything, I owe you something. I mean you and Mr. Pepe are always so nice, the friendliest people in this whole building." He places himself very close to Joseph, who shifts his weight to his back foot in order to gain space without offending him.

"Take the actress on the sixth floor, for example. What's the big deal, a stupid kiddie show! I mean, so what if she's popular with the preteens? So what if my nieces are crazy about her? She and her lousy friends have no right to treat us doormen like dirt. Or how about the lady lawyer one floor down? She calls all of us 'young man.' She doesn't know a single one of our names. Dr. Vardi's kids are the worst, though. We're always getting called up there to save them from some disaster and they never thank us, never give us one little word of appreciation. They act like it's what we owe 'em, but even if you say it's all part of our job—which it isn't—but let's say it is, well, it still wouldn't hurt to say thank you the way you guys do. That's what I'll take away from this job with me when I move on—to remember the little people who make your life more comfortable and tell them, 'Hey, man, you're great. Keep up the good work.' That's all it takes."

Joseph considers counting the bottles of beer in the cartons. He has never seen Shlomi so animated. Is it just the approaching weekend, the end of his shift, the release of two buttons on a uniform?

Shlomi runs a hand through his hair, fingers spread wide, and takes a deep breath. He takes another and then a third before Joseph feels compelled to speak. "Is something wrong, Shlomi? Is there something I can do for you?"

The doorman seems to be staring at a high point on the far wall. "I was thinking more like what it was *I* could do for *you*." He takes another deep breath and stares at Joseph.

"Are you talking about odd jobs to earn some pocket money?"

"I was thinking of something more personal," Shlomi answers, staring again at some faraway spot.

Joseph looks more closely at Shlomi now, noticing and appraising the young man Pepe has always found "attractive, in a primitive way." There is nothing refined in his features, his jaw thrust forward and always shadowed dark with stubble. His nose is fleshy and his eyebrows nearly meet along a brow so prominent it gives him a look of constant brooding. But it is a reliable face, the face of a man you can trust.

For an instant Joseph imagines Shlomi's heavy young body in bed. Hairy, sweaty, eager, and energetic. Willing to please and be pleasured. Isn't he worried what his fellow doormen will think about his visiting the penthouse? Surely they know where he is; every minute longer is further confirmation of their suspicions. Is it money he is after, an easy life? Or has curiosity, desire, or an adventurous spirit overtaken him?

Joseph is aroused at the prospect, but just then another thought grips and shakes him. Shlomi is Noam's age, or Ethan's. A young man searching, innocent; someone's son. His own sons will be here in this very flat in just a few hours.

"You're a fine man, Shlomi. Pepe and I are both fond of you and I'm glad you recognize our respect and appreciation for all you do for us. But there's no room for changing our relationship in any way, and it would certainly not help you in life." Joseph is proud of the gentle rebuff.

"Please, Professor Licht, try me," the doorman pleads in a near whimper. "You won't be disappointed." He slips two more buttons through their holes then reaches down to his crotch.

Joseph grabs both of Shlomi's hands and brings them to his face. "Shlomi, don't do this. You will find someone suitable, someone your age who understands what you want and need. Maybe not tomorrow or the next day, but be patient and wait for the right person, whoever that may be." He releases Shlomi's hands and pushes him gently away. "Now go," he says. "Enjoy your time off. I'll tell you all about my family reunion on Sunday."

With Shlomi's departure, Joseph's spirits lift. He is flattered by the young doorman's advances, mercenary though they may have been, and pleased with his own artful handling of this tricky affair. He is especially relieved that Shlomi approached him and not Pepe.

*

After covering and refrigerating the cooled food, Joseph checks the answering machine. Nothing. He reviews his to-do list. The queen-sized bed for Gidi and his wife still worries him. The building superintendent has secured a single mattress that Joseph can stow behind the door of that bedroom, in case the couple is in the period of *niddah*, when they are forbidden to one another. Perhaps he should switch them to the other guest bedroom after all, the one with the twin beds separated by a chest of drawers. But it seems such a shame to separate them if they are in fact permitted to one another, and besides, he supposes he cannot very well put his other sons in a bed together, so the sleeping plan stays as it is.

Joseph circles through all the bedrooms, inspecting each well-made bed, and places a tiny chocolate basket filled with speckled jelly beans on each pillow. He recalls the Hasidic story about a childless couple told by their *rebbe* to purchase a baby carriage as a sign of faith that God will eventually respond to their prayers. Joseph cannot bear to believe that one of his boys will not be with him this weekend, so he has gone diligently through all the motions of preparing for a full house. At the queen-size bed he stops and sits abruptly, clutching a pillow to his chest. He is worried and his mind floats and drifts.

Joseph rises too quickly from the edge of the bed and swoons a bit before catching himself. His refrigerator is full of food, the kitchen is clean, the dining-room table set for seven, the beds and bathrooms topped up with fresh linens and towels. He has considered every detail and made a thousand small decisions over several weeks to reach this point. Now all that remains for him to do is flip a few switches to usher his home from clean and organized to Sabbath-ready, and then, more difficult than all the shopping and cooking and cleaning and fretting, to push himself, warily, into Shabbat. Joseph prays—to himself, to the sky, perhaps to the clock on the kitchen wall—that this last hour of solitude before his sons begin to arrive will pass slowly and with dignity, and that it will bring him some measure of peace and wisdom and clarity.

kodesh *(holy, sacred, sanctified; the Sabbath)*

FRIDAY, MARCH 1 — SATURDAY, MARCH 2, 1996

JOSEPH STARES FROM THE depths of a pillowed armchair pulled close to the sliding glass doors of the terrace at the dark orange sun that has plunged through the thick ceiling of gray clouds, well on its descent into evening. His senses seem to have abandoned their usual posts and gone to carouse with one another: the orange of the sun roars in his ears, he can see the scent of simmering soup wafting from the kitchen, and a melody he cannot name leaves a peculiar salty taste on his lips and tongue. A crinkled letter lies splayed across his lap.

In the last hour his sons and daughter-in-law arrived and then, before he could finish showering, deserted him for services at an ultra-Orthodox synagogue of Gidi's bidding. He had felt unhinged at the first knock and staggered to the front door in a stupor of emotions at what he might find on the other side. He was met by a large luggage cart crammed full of crumpled shopping bags and cardboard boxes, clothes on hangers, and two small and battered suitcases. A newish doorman, whose name escaped Joseph, stood to the side, his face pulled into a look of surprised amusement.

"Good afternoon, sir." The doorman hesitated, waiting for a sign from Joseph that he was indeed delivering this unlikely baggage and the guests who went with it to the right place.

"Well, yes, good afternoon, young man. Come in, come in. Let's get these deposited as quickly as possible." Only as the cart rolled past him did Joseph catch sight of his youngest son, Gidi, and his bride standing motionless between the elevator and a towering potted palm.

When Gidi was five he had filched one of his older brothers' bicycles for a cruise down the sloping road that led from the family home past the moshav's citrus groves and ended at the village cemetery. But the bike had hand brakes—a mechanism Gidi did not yet know existed—so his furious backpedaling did nothing to stop him or even slow him down. In the ensuing crash he lost two baby teeth, mangled his chin, and suffered a medium-deep gash over his left eye. That cigar-shaped scar, still present on his twenty-two-year-old face, reassured Joseph that this was, in fact, his son. Gidi had been a robust child, nearly chubby, but now, encased in the shin-length double-breasted black coat of the ultra-Orthodox, he looked somehow depleted, long and thin like a stick of licorice. The only color in his face was the flush that came from wearing too many clothes in an overheated building. His beard—blond and boyish, a scraggly fuzz that barely straddled his jawbone—made him look more Amish than Jewish.

Batya was a pleasant surprise. Her eyebrows gave her away as a redhead, even though Joseph could not see a single hair on her meticulously covered head. He imagined her to have been a beautiful child, with a mane of wild hair the color of a summer sunset in a rush of wind behind her as she ran and played and squealed with life and energy. She, too, was quite thin, causing Joseph to wonder whether they ate enough; surely they would enjoy the meals he had prepared, and he would send food home with them, too. Batya was the first to break their stunned silence.

"Shalom, Professor Licht," she said in a breathless, child-like voice as she took a small step in his general direction.

She did not seem to know how to continue, but Joseph rescued her, saying, "I'm so glad we finally meet, Batya," and he really did feel glad. "Please come in. And do call me Joseph."

Batya followed Gidi, who had not yet uttered a word. Joseph showed them and the doorman to their room, a bright, frivolous explosion of pastel prints and lace with plush pillows and a wildflower quilt on the queen-size bed. Joseph noted the flicker of joy on Batya's face and followed her gaze to a framed snapshot of the twins at their fourth birthday party, her husband nearly twenty years earlier.

"This won't do." Gidi addressed this comment to the bed or the luggage cart; Joseph was not quite sure which. The doorman stopped unloading the luggage cart mid-bend.

"We'll need an extra room." Gidi did not elaborate. Joseph looked to Batya but her head was bent and her face offered no explanation, only humiliation. The doorman straightened, looking to Joseph for instruction.

"The superintendent has promised to bring up an extra

mattress, if that's the problem. . . ." Joseph said this under his breath, eager to avoid embarrassing his daughter-in-law.

"An extra mattress won't do. We need an extra room." Gidi's face had reddened, causing the cigar-shaped scar to fade.

Joseph felt a sudden longing for Pepe, a solid presence to whom he could anchor himself. His brain felt like an elevator jammed between floors. He could no better reassess the bedroom assignments than deal with the fact that his son had not yet said hello, only barked a complaint. What to address first? He was formulating answers to these questions when he realized that Gidi was busy instructing the doorman to replace a number of the boxes and bags on the luggage cart and wheel them to the kitchen. Surely he did not plan to sleep in there?

Joseph mutely followed the two men, leaving Batya rooted to the guest bedroom floor. He knew she would enjoy the room as soon as her husband relaxed.

Gidi took one look around the cavernous kitchen, removed a large towel from one of the bags, and placed it on the cooking island in the middle of the room, indicating to the doorman he could unload there. The doorman did not wait for Joseph to agree, sensing who was boss at the moment.

A whole kitchen emerged from the luggage cart: plates, serving dishes, utensils, vegetables in plastic bags, loaves of challah, wine, a hot plate. Salt and pepper shakers, a thermos, hand towels. A store-bought cake in an aluminum baking tin.

Joseph briskly dismissed the doorman through the service entrance, forgetting to tip him. He composed himself before speaking, wishing to sound rational, not hurt or insulted. "I've kashered the kitchen, bought and toiveled new cookery and cutlery, purchased and prepared everything according to your standards of kashrut." He lowered his voice to avoid sounding shrill. "Do you mean to tell me that you plan to eat your own food at my dinner table?"

Gidi addressed his father for the first time. "We could eat alone in the kitchen and save us all a lot of discomfort."

Just then the buzzer rang, the other doorman announcing the arrival of two more guests. Joseph reprimanded him, in a low, threatening hiss from the kitchen intercom: "I left clear instructions not to detain my sons with your exaggerated security." He was nearly choked with anger. "Send them up right away!" He wheeled around without looking at Gidi and strode to the front door. Out in the hallway he took several deep breaths, then checked his composure in the mirror. By the time Daniel and Ethan reached his floor he had returned to a forced equilibrium, managing a smile for his two eldest sons.

Ethan returned Joseph's smile; Daniel did not. Ethan's small, flattened backpack fell to the floor as he hugged his father. Joseph knew better than to expect the same from Daniel. Instead he squeezed Daniel's shoulder and pulled him into the apartment.

The boys went to greet Gidi, and Joseph, returning to the guest room, found Batya shoeless, awash in a sea of lace and plump pillows, examining the photograph of her husband from a different life. She sprang to a sitting position when he entered, tucking her stockinged legs under the quilted blanket. Joseph ignored this, hoping to make her feel more comfortable. He resolved to let her sleep in this most feminine of rooms no matter what her husband might decide, despite the waste of a bed when they would be so pressed for space.

"How could you tell them apart?" Her freckled forehead

wrinkled with worry lines, her thin, gingery eyebrows like two circumflexes over cinnamon brown eyes.

Joseph's lips curved into a small smile as he contemplated the sweet, innocent face before him. He could not resist the thought that even their attempts at neutralizing their good looks would not prevent Batya and Gidi from producing anything but gorgeous children. "Well, their mother never had a problem, but they could certainly fool me," he said in a warmly conspiratorial tone.

Batya forgot her reticence and unfolded her legs. "I wanted to paint them each a different color," she said, pointing to her toenails, "but my husband wouldn't let me. Only clear nail polish. Even though nobody would ever see my toes." She blushed and smiled, looking up at Joseph. "Well, almost nobody."

"Don't worry. I'm your father-in-law. Almost nobody."

"Yes, that's right," she said, nodding, wide eyed.

Ethan appeared in the doorway. "Hello, Batya," he said with a big, warm smile. "Everything all set for Shabbat, Dad? Lights, timers, hot plates? Have you put out precut toilet paper? Did you open the seals on the wine bottles? Gidi wants to know which of the outlets in the kitchen are on the Shabbat timer. He's setting up his own hot plate."

Joseph excused himself and headed back toward the kitchen, with Ethan close behind. As he passed through the living room he ran into Gidi's twin, Gavriel, just entering the front door. Gavri's beard was neater than Gidi's and his face fuller. Ritual *tzitzit* fringes hung long from the white shirt flowing loose from his belt. "Shalom, Father," he said politely.

"Hey, little brother!" Ethan had always been Gavri's

buddy, his chief defender against Daniel, who usually took Gidi's side in fights. "We missed you at the station."

"Don't people in Tel Aviv listen to the news? There was a shooting incident in Hebron this afternoon and the roads were blocked for more than an hour. I missed the last bus from Jerusalem and thought about turning around and going home. I knew you'd kill me, though, so I caught a ride with this weird old couple. Well, never mind. I made it here; that's what's important."

Gidi's superkosher corner in the kitchen reminded Joseph of the shrines in miniature he had seen in the Far East: choice delicacies in small quantities offered to the gods, everything laid out in perfect rows or at right angles. He has his grandfather's German love of order, Joseph thought. Gidi would have a fit at these comparisons: Buddhists and Germans, idol worshippers and Jew murderers. Joseph would share these musings with no one, since his other sons would be offended and come to the defense of their little brother, while Pepe would agree only too quickly, forcing Joseph to explain and justify his son's odd behavior. He showed Gideon what he needed to know, flipped the switches on several Shabbat timers, and called Batya to show her the candlesticks he had arranged for her in the dining room.

He enjoyed the hustle and bustle of last-minute Shabbat preparations with his sons and his new daughter-in-law, even though he recognized their teamwork for what it was: an illusion, the lot of them thrown together but not truly together, colliding, interacting, but separate. He worried as the sun dipped dangerously low to the horizon and Noam had not yet arrived.

When Joseph announced he was going to shower no one responded. He was glad to be in his bathroom, behind a locked door where he could undress or cry or hide his weary, worried face in his hands. They will warm up; the meal will melt them, he told himself. Gideon and Batya can eat what they like. Who cares?

It took a moment for Joseph to hear the pounding through the torrent of hot water coursing its way from the crown of his head to the tips of his toes. He shut off the water and listened. "Father, Noam's downstairs, just in from Spain. We're all going to some *shtiebl* that Gidi has picked out for us to pray at. So Shabbat Shalom."

Joseph did not respond. Not because he did not know which son was speaking to him. Not because he knew it was improper to offer Sabbath greetings in the nude, from the shower. It was because they were sneaking out. So they were embarrassed to sit with their father in a shul? He would have been happy to go if asked, had convinced himself during the course of the afternoon that he should accompany them to the local synagogue. He would even have agreed to this hovel of black-hatted ultra-Orthodox; that would not have scared him off. But they had planned it without him, left without inviting him. Joseph had not even had a second to acknowledge Noam's arrival, which meant the five of them would be present, all his sons on hand for the celebration.

He waited until he was sure they were gone before emerging from the shower. He put on the pale yellow oxford shirt he had ironed earlier, the staid blue trousers. He unfolded his white *kipa*, the one he had worn at his wedding, but he did not place it on his head. Not yet. He would wait until they returned, until they said the blessings over the wine and the bread. He would suffer his freedom until the last possible minute.

"Sixteen floors. This is going to be a lot of fun to climb back up."

When the elevator spills Daniel, Ethan, Gavri, Gidi, and Batya into the lobby, they find Noam with his back to the guards' desk, a tall blonde in a Lycra dress and strappy heels pressed up close to him. The guards on duty are too entranced by Noam and the blonde to notice the arrival of the rest of the Licht family.

"No, I never promised I would call." Noam's voice is steady and quiet, as though they have been through this several times already. "In fact, I wanted to call, but you wrote your number on some little scrap of paper I put through the laundry."

"You are so cute," she says with a malicious passion as she leans in to place a short kiss on his lips. Her heels clack as she slinks toward the front door, clearly aware that Noam and the guards and all these people who have stepped off the elevator are watching her. The guard nearest the entrance remembers his duty too late and leaps up to open the door only when her hand is already poised to push it. She lets him sweep it open for her, then turns to face Noam. "Your driver's license. I wrote it on the back of your driver's license. Don't bother to call unless you can find a *serious* way to make it up to me. I mean true *groveling*, not just a silly bouquet of flowers or some stale chocolates. Ta!" She throws a bright, sassy smile to Noam and a wave to the rest of the crowd and disappears into the street.

"Jeez, I don't even remember her name," says Noam, shaking his head.

"Ah, don't bother," says the stouter of the two doormen. "She lives with an old geezer on the eighth floor. A real bitch, if you'll excuse me. Pretends she's a lady, but she tossed the old guy's kids out and now she cheats on him."

"Shut up, Coby," says the other guard. "Don't talk about the residents that way. Don't talk about them at all, in fact."

"Hi, everybody. Sorry." Noam hugs each brother in turn, but catches himself before embracing his off-limits sister-in-law. "Dad's not coming with us?"

No one answers.

"All right, let's go to shul."

Out on the street they jostle one another, bumping shoulders and arms. Gidi leads the way to a *shtiebl*, the tiny makeshift synagogue of an ultra-Orthodox sect whose aged rebbe lives in the center of Tel Aviv, the heart and soul of Israeli hedonism. His followers are known for their fierce piety, the eyes of the men permanently cast downward to avoid gazing upon tempting Tel Avivans. Batya is the only one trying to keep pace, dutifully following several paces behind her husband. Ethan and Gavri talk seriously about the recent bombings, the situation in Lebanon, Israel in the wake of Prime Minister Rabin's assassination. Noam and Daniel stroll more leisurely at the rear. Daniel listens while Noam attempts to sort out the intricacies of his current relationships, but as the names and events pile up, Daniel's thoughts float to the lonely young Indian woman from the start of his day. Gidi makes frantic hand signals to encourage his brothers to walk faster, and at the corner of Nordau and Ibn Gvirol streets he turns to shout at them, his face pink with effort and anger. "We'll be late for *minha* prayers! Hurry or we'll miss *minha*!" he sputters, his voice a high, tight squeak.

Batya tries to concentrate on walking quickly by fixing her eyes on the heels of her husband's black shoes, but she is distracted by so much of what she sees in the shop windows and hears from balconies and gardens that she finds herself falling behind time and again. Worse, by far, are the wonderful scents that float past her: simmering chicken soup, breaded schnitzels frying in their pans, a late-baked braided bread loaf encrusted with slightly singed raisins. Tel Aviv has gone quiet, the lull when the Friday brunchers and shoppers—who only several hours earlier had crammed the sidewalk cafés on Shenkin Street and the arts and crafts stalls in Nahalat Binyamin—are home resting in preparation for late-night raids on sushi bars, Arab grills in Jaffa, and countless dimly lit pubs and trendy discos that dot the city like poppy seeds on a challah. The only people they pass are older men in skullcaps and Sabbath finery, rushing this way or that to the synagogue of their choice. No one exchanges greetings.

A musky twilight has settled on the city by the time they reach the *shtiebl*. Inside the front door, next to a hat rack upon which hang several rows of identical fur-trimmed *shtreimls*, the men part company with Batya, who ascends a dark stairway to the women's section. Downstairs, forty or fifty men and boys, all in striped frock coats, shiny black knickers, and white stockings, are engaged in prayer or study, rocking, swaying, reading. Several tug at their beards and one or two chat in low whispers while the cantor intones the end of the *minha* service, his prayers punctuated with periodic "*aw-meyns*" from the congregation in their Yiddish lilt. Gidi rushes to a half-empty row near the front and breaks immediately into a speed sway, as if he can make up for being late by rocking faster and harder than anyone else in the *shtiebl*. Ethan joins him, rocking at a slower pace. Gavri, who has already prayed *minha*, selects a Bible from the shelves and stands next to Ethan, reading. Daniel and Noam remain in the back, by the wall. Noam pats the top of his head where the curls grow thickest, checking to make sure the skullcap he clipped there as he entered his father's building is still hanging on. He leans toward his brother. "I live ten minutes from here, in another world and a different century," he says quietly, shaking his head.

A freckled teenager with curled orange sidelocks shushes him.

Noam glares at the freckled boy. "Look up there," he says to Daniel, pointing toward the women's section, a tiny room overhanging the men's section, its window obscured by a metal grate and a heavy curtain. "They couldn't possibly see anything from behind all that. Air wouldn't even pass through," he says in disbelief. The freckled boy gets up and moves to a spot on the other side of the room.

The service is long and slow. At its conclusion, the rebbe, a stooped ancient with a wispy beard that makes him look more like a wizened Chinese sage than a wise old Jew, rises to address the crowd. There is complete silence in the small room and all books are quietly closed; no one will dare sneak a read now. The men all lean forward and cup their ears to catch the rebbe's parched wisdom, which pops from his mouth in dry, wooden bubbles. His voice fails; his eyes water; he gazes past the heads of his loyal followers at nothing; he seems to forget what he started to say, but he continues for twenty minutes, maybe thirty. No one stirs or grows restless except for one or two members of the Licht family. When he sits down at last, midsentence, or rather midgurgle, the room erupts into song. Chairs and tables are moved aside to make room for dancing. Gidi, Gavri, and Ethan join the circle of dancers. Noam leaves the room but Daniel remains leaning against the wall, his mouth forming a small smile that grows slightly larger and warmer as Ethan dances by with a shrug, as if to explain his bewilderment.

Batya is standing alone outside the *shtiebl*, huddled in her coat, when Noam joins her. "*Gut Shabbes*," she says, looking down.

"Shabbat Shalom to you, too," he responds, relieved to be in the cold night air. He glances up and down the quiet street, aware that there is no traffic, almost no noise at all apart from the low rush and hum of a city after dark.

Noam sighs heavily then says to the sky, "That was really something." He catches Batya looking at him, her mouth slightly ajar, like a child of five watching the performing lions at a circus, all curiosity and fear. "Do you go to a synagogue like that one?" he asks her.

"Oh," she answers breathlessly, "ours is much bigger." She nods vigorously and seems pleased to have been asked something to which she knows the single correct response.

"But, I mean, do the women sit behind an iron wall there, too?"

She smiles, indulging a question only a child would ask. "It's not a wall. We can hear through it just fine!"

"Do most women come to shul or do they wait for their husbands at home?"

"Mothers and grandmothers stay home, for sure, but the older girls go to shul to pray."

She pauses and bites her bottom lip as if trying to prevent what she is about to say. Noam looks into her pale, round face, waiting patiently for her to continue.

"The married women who have not yet been blessed with children go to shul to pray, too," she says quietly.

He considers how different she is from the women he knows, all bristling with confidence, strong-headed and focused. Their perfumes, their hairstyles, their lacy silk panties and executive suits share a common cri de coeur: take me as I am, love me the way I want; my needs are just as important as yours, my desires of equal worth. But this child-woman, his own and only sister-in-law, what is her breed? What is her species? A wisp of her hair, bright orange even in the glazed light of a street lamp, has escaped from the carefully wrapped scarf on her head, and though he does not dare do it, Noam has the overwhelming urge to tuck it gently back into place and cup her soft, freckled cheek in the palm of his hand. Instead, he says sotto voce, in a tone usually reserved for low whispers of love, "And I'm certain God will answer their prayers."

Batya is instantly elated, as though Noam, the family apostate, has some inside track to the truth, a private and personal relationship with God himself. "Yes, God willing!" she says, flushing. "I'm certain, too!"

Daniel appears in the doorway, silent. The *shtiebl* empties quickly. Men and boys in fur *shtreimls* gush into the street like beavers in a river. Ethan and the twins are among the last to emerge.

"Now that's what I call a great service," says Gidi, more loudly than necessary. He nods to his wife, then both look away.

Ethan looks to his eldest brother, Daniel, then claps his hands. "All right, gentlemen and lady, let's get going. We've got a long walk back and Father is probably already wondering what's happened to us."

"Who cares what Father thinks?" Gidi says dismissively. "I don't want to get back there any sooner than necessary."

"He's gone to a lot of trouble and this is really important to him," says Gavri. "I think it's the least we can do for him."

"After all he's done for us?"

"It doesn't matter who or what he is," Gavri tells his twin and his other brothers. "He's still our father and we owe him a certain amount of respect. That's the only reason I'm here this weekend."

"And to see all of us, of course," adds Ethan.

They walk in a group now, the streets still drained of people.

"Anyone seen Mother lately?" Noam asks offhandedly.

"I stopped over and had a nap there this morning on the way down from Lebanon," Ethan says, proud to exert his primacy in this field. Then he adds quickly, "And Daniel was there this morning, too."

Gavri scowls. "I meant to call. All day I kept thinking I would get to it but I never did. Gosh, am I a loser sometimes."

"She looked a little funny to me," Ethan says, "and she kept avoiding me whenever I tried to talk about it with her."

"What do you mean 'funny'?" asks Gavri.

"Misshapen or something. Almost like she's pregnant."

"That would be something, wouldn't it?" says Gidi. "A little brother for us all, or maybe at long last a sister. Batya's aunt gave birth to her seventeenth child on her fiftieth birthday, so I guess it's not impossible."

Noam slaps him on the back, chuckling. "Batya's aunt probably had a husband at the time."

Gavri laughs louder and longer than Noam. "Maybe it's Grandfather's baby! Maybe this kid will be our brother and our cousin!"

Daniel stops walking and turns to Gavri. His eyes have narrowed to slits and his fists are clenched at his sides. "Shut up already with your nonsense! Don't ever say anything like that again!"

Daniel walks ahead while the other boys and Batya linger for a moment. When he is out of earshot Ethan says glumly, "You guys don't remember what it was like when Father left and the kids in school used to tease us. We were the only boys without a father, except for Meir Cohen. But his father was killed in the Yom Kippur War, so he was a hero. We were freaks. Worse yet, there was this disgusting rumor about Mother and Grandfather that went around school—around the whole village, in fact. Bina Hartog actually came up to Daniel and me at the greengrocer's and asked if it was true that Father had left because Mother and Grandfather were . . . in love." He stops, surveying his brothers' reactions. Noam is watching Daniel, already a block away from them. Gavri and Batya, repelled and fascinated, wait wide eyed for more. Gidi is holding his sides as if in pain. "I didn't really understand then what she was talking about, but I understood it was quite bad. Bad enough to make Daniel ram a shopping cart into her and knock her into a big stack of egg cartons. He really banged her up pretty bad, and there were broken eggs everywhere, and Motty, who was the owner then, told him never to set foot inside the shop again. And you know it's the only shop in the village. I thought that punishment was much worse than what Daniel had done to Bina. He ran out crying and didn't come home until well after dark. And he didn't go back to the greengrocer's for years and years. Remember how he would send us in, Noam, and make us describe what was in the sweets section and then send us back again with the cash to make the purchase? Do you remember what he always said?"

"'I'll beat you to dust if you so much as take a whiff of my candy,'" Noam says without a smile. Daniel has turned a corner and is out of his sight. "Enough of this. Let's go to Father's," he says.

All the light has been sucked out of the sky by the sun, which has disappeared beneath the horizon. The boys are late. The food has been heating too long and heavy clouds are gliding swiftly inland over the water. What is keeping them? Joseph wonders. There may be a downpour before they make it back.

Joseph stares ahead at his reflection in the glass doors of the terrace, a man alone, dwarfed in his chair, waiting for his tardy guests. He and his house are now ready. It is dark and quiet; the Sabbath queen has arrived in her cloak of heavy silence. Suddenly Joseph no longer feels like fussing over the meal. He does not care if the wine is breathing or the hot plate has overheated the food. He tries to remember why this reunion meant so much to him. Pepe warned him, said his sons would be ungrateful. Is he to expect a whole weekend of being snubbed?

For fortification, or retreat, Joseph gathers the sheets of paper in his lap and reads.

Dearest Love,

I am saturated with the love of our last meeting, as though the bones and blood and tissue have been removed from my body and replaced with pure light, a holy radiance suffused with the breath of angels. I feel it swirling inside me, frothing; it makes me light and buoyant, I am a bubble on a wave, a butterfly on a breeze. I see only stars and moonlight, hear only symphonies. I cannot work, I have no need for sleep, no desire for food, but when I do read or taste or dream it is always you that my ears or tongue or heart wishes to recapture. I have sought out G-d my whole life and followed His commandments carefully, inviting them to permeate every waking hour of my every day, as it is said, Remember all G-d's commandments and perform them. But I have never known such joy, such elation of spirit as I do today. J'avais réduit mon âme à une seule mélodie, plaintive et monotone; j'avais fait de ma vie du silence, où ne devait monter qu'un psaume. And what did that psalm say? Put not your trust in princes, nor in the son of man, in whom there is no help. His breath goes forth, he returns to his earth; in that very day his thoughts perish. But what are you, Joseph, if not G-d's very essence? Only through you can I feel His presence like a second soul juxtaposed with my own, only through you can I understand His highest attribute: love. It is clear to me through the love we have created together that this was His intention all along, that we know each other in order to know Him, that our spiritual and physical love is the love He feels for all creation. And so we honor Him by loving one another:

Desire of my heart and delight of my eyes . . .
Rise and feed me with the honey of your lips, and satisfy me.
I will be ravished by your beauty—G-d is there!

*I have vaulted over the River Jordan with my lance and found
a new world there: your love and G-d's love. I am profound-
ly altered and deeply grateful.*

Yours eternally

Joseph did not know that this would be the only letter he
would ever receive from Yoel. At first he did not scrutinize
the letter, asked no questions of it. He was enchanted, enrap-
tured, a prisoner of its mellifluence, a fly caught in its sticky
honey. He noted, of course, that the letter was not expressly
addressed to him, nor was it signed; however, Joseph understood that their precarious position—the danger inherent in
their relationship—required such precautions.

But in the years without Yoel, in his absence and in the
absence of any other letters to balance or explain it, Joseph
has made a study of this one missive, has spent time deciphering it, twisting it, turning it, standing it on its head,
climbing into its syntax; in his dreams he has kissed and fon-
dled the words, tossed them in the air, rolled them into a pillow to sleep on, sucked them like hard candies. But in all
those years he has never swallowed them, never could. He
has tracked them to their sources and discovered their roots.
And what he has found is nothing more than a man in thrall,
a man who had discovered his own body and had touched,
for the first time, his own desire, and with his new knowledge had ceased to believe all he had believed before. Worse,
he had stolen from the treasure of his tremendous knowledge
to pay the price of that desire.

Joseph recognized several of Yoel's references without
acknowledging them on his first reading. They aroused his

suspicions to his beloved's distortions, but only many months later, when he was adapting to his new life and could afford to spare a corner of his battered soul for reflection, did he pursue the issue. Why, for instance, had Yoel pointed out that he had spent his life remembering God's commandments and performing them while ignoring the rest of the verse: . . . *and do not wander after your heart and your eyes after which you may stray?* How could he mock the advice of the psalmist never to put his trust in human beings when that very trust would trip them both up such a short time later?

Yoel's nod to the Talmudic story of Resh Lakish at the River Jordan proved more puzzling. Here was a sinner, a Romanized Jew, who had stripped off his clothes and vaulted the river for carnal reasons—the sight of the exceedingly beautiful Rabbi Yohanan!—but was spiritually transformed by the experience; returned, as it were, to tradition, law, and study. How could Yoel compare himself to a Jewish thief, a sometime gladiator, steeped in the pleasures of Rome, delivered late to the hand of God? Was Yoel not Resh Lakish's very antithesis?

After this frightful revelation Joseph set out in pursuit of the other two sources, possessed with deciphering the mystery Yoel had left him: had Yoel purposefully, blasphemously, plundered his knowledge, distorting what he knew in order to justify his relationship with Joseph? Or was he naively discovering new meanings in words he had always known? The fragment of poem in his letter proffered clues through language and imagery. A thick volume of medieval Spanish Jewish poetry that Joseph found in a dimly lit section of the university library yielded a whole series of poems written by the greatest poets of the era—Yehuda HaLevi, Shlomo Ibn

Gvirol, Moshe Ibn Ezra—to and about young men they fancied. The one Yoel quoted was by Ibn Ezra, but here he had clearly selected exactly what suited him, omitting the rest:

> Desire of my heart and delight of my eyes . . .
> Many admonish me, but I do not heed;
> Come, O gazelle, and I will subdue them.
> Time will destroy them and death shepherd them.
> Come, O gazelle, rise and feed me
> With the honey of your lips, and satisfy me.
> Why do they hold back my heart, why?
> If because of sin and guilt,
> I will be ravished by your beauty—God is there!

In Yoel's condensed version the admonishers were abolished. Gone, too, were the sin and guilt. Yoel had dispensed with the unpleasantries and left intact the beauty and the passion. Joseph could not rid himself of the thought that if Yoel had only been able to acknowledge the critics and the sin and the guilt he might have been able to live with them. Long before Joseph finally found and deciphered Yoel's French quote in an English translation of Marguerite Yourcenar's *Alexis*, borrowed from a colleague, he knew all he needed to draw his conclusions: the sum of Yoel's cheap and unworthy distortions was a huge deception; he had cheated all those involved in the relationship—himself, Joseph, and God.

Just as he thinks that the last of his resolve and energy have dropped away like beads from a broken necklace, Joseph holds in a deep breath, then lets it seep slowly out. He begins collecting those beads one by one. *I have reached fifty in excellent health. I live in a beautiful home with a man who cares deeply for me. I am respected in my field. I have made difficult choices in my life. I have tried to be fair with everyone.* His breathing has quickened again and he feels color rushing to his cheeks. *I love my sons and I will love my daughter-in-law. I have given them the most precious gift a parent can give: the support to become exactly who and what they wish to be.* He hears the door to the stairwell creak open. *I will not let them ruin my celebration in my own home.* He stands, bracing himself to greet them.

Joseph does not gently prod his family into the dining room as he might with other guests. He precedes them so that he can watch their reactions as they enter. Indeed, the room has an effect. The wood and silver gleam in pools of yellow light, the crystal catches and refracts the thousand tiny blazes from the chandelier, and the china is polished to such a shine that it mirrors the fresco on the ceiling. Huge oil paintings and massive furniture dwarf his guests. They are subdued and compliant as Joseph establishes the seating arrangement: the twins and Batya on one side of the table, Ethan and Noam facing them, and Daniel at its head facing Joseph at the foot, closest to the kitchen. They struggle with their tall, carved chairs. Batya throws a suspicious backward glance at the English hunting scene on the wall behind her, as if to make sure the hounds in the foreground have not moved any closer.

Joseph begins to relax as his sons sing "Peace Be Upon You," though he is baffled by their preference for their grandfather's German tune and not the more Israeli, minor-key melody they insisted on as children. He joins them for the second verse. Only Batya is silent. Her eyes are closed and she sways to the chanting of so many men, but she does not open her mouth. *Kol b'isha ervah*, he suddenly remembers, the prohibition against hearing a woman's singing voice in public.

Batya's brown button eyes open wide at the start of "A Woman of Valor." This time she does not sway. Her face tilts over her plate and she seems in pain at being singled out, keenly aware of her only-woman status at the table. But Joseph doubts whether any of these men, even her husband, is singing to her. He assumes it is Rebecca who visits their thoughts, as she does his. She once told the boys, when she and Joseph were still married, that this was the payment owed her for a week's toil; that all those meals, all those loads of laundry, all those words of support and hours of help with homework and bandaged knees and clean diapers could be paid off by singing her this one song, with intent and emotion, before the start of the Sabbath evening meal. To this day, Ethan has told Joseph, she insists on this serenade by whichever of her sons is on hand. What Joseph does not tell his sons is that these are the very words he included in the letter he put on her pillow when he left home that last time.

By mutual consent Gidi is chosen to make the blessing over the wine. Joseph is silent as his ultra-Orthodox son rejects the ornate Turkish silver *kiddush* cup and the fine merlot, fetching his own cup and wine from the kitchen. He speaks the blessing rather than singing it, using Yiddish inflections and pronunciation instead of Hebrew. Joseph winces and wonders how his father tolerates Gidi's vexatious visits. He is relieved when they have finished laving their hands and have made the blessing over the bread. Now he is in control of the evening and, he feels certain, the atmosphere will loosen up and become more enjoyable from course to course.

They are discussing the synagogue service when Joseph reenters the dining room with the hors d'oeuvres on a large silver tray. Self-consciously he announces the course in French but his guests are all listening to Noam. "Who can possibly understand the prayers in that accent?" Noam is asking.

"The words are not so much the point," counters Gidi. Joseph pauses at the note of passion in his voice, glad to hear that something has finally shaken him from his angry silence. "It's a whole ambiance. Couldn't you feel the energy in that room, the intense love of the Holy Name and all his creatures?"

Noam frowns. His voice is slightly louder this time. "What about those creatures who drive on the Sabbath? 'Shabbes! Shabbes!' your friends shout at them as they pelt them with stones. Is that love?"

"It's hard to sit by and watch people err," answers Gidi, looking around the table.

"Bon appetit," Joseph calls out cheerfully, then disappears again into the kitchen. Had any of his sons offered assistance Joseph would have waved him back to his seat. Each course stands ready to be served; there is almost nothing left to organize. Besides, the kitchen is his kingdom and his refuge. There is no conspiratorial feeling here, just a contented hush that Joseph appreciates now more than ever.

He is doubly glad to be alone in the kitchen when he opens the refrigerator and discovers he has forgotten to turn

off the light inside. Wasn't this small but crucial chore included on his list? Without wasting a second he shifts the light
switch to *off* and closes the door. Had Gidi seen him, he
would no doubt have forbidden his father and everyone else
from opening the refrigerator for the entire Sabbath. Joseph's
meals would have been reduced to farcical improvisations of
what should have been an outstanding culinary experience.
While taking three deep breaths to calm his nerves before
serving the soup he wonders what other Shabbat rituals he
has neglected, what other Shabbat rules he will need to break
to steer them safely through the weekend.

All seven Lichts eat their soup in silence. No one requests
seconds. Noam, needing an excuse to leave the room, comes to
help Joseph bring the main dishes to the table. "It was worse
than you could imagine. Be glad you didn't come." Still distraught by the ultra-Orthodox service, he does not whisper.
Joseph shushes him.

"How can the women stand it, or the men for that matter?" Noam is pacing the far end of the kitchen while Joseph
loads food onto trays. "If the services weren't bad enough,
the speech at the end was sickening. This ancient rabbi ram-
bles on for half an hour. I could understand about one-tenth
of what he was saying. Then, when he finishes, everyone
starts dancing and singing like madmen. It turned my stomach to watch them all in that frenzy."

Joseph does not wish to take sides. He and Noam can
agree on this point only when the other boys are not around.
More than anything, he wishes to maintain an ambiance of
tranquillity this weekend. So he says lightly, as he removes a
casserole from the hot plate, "Let's try and keep the peace

around here, shall we? Even if we don't necessarily agree with everything." He delivers the food to the dining room before Noam can respond.

A few minutes later, finally seated, Joseph is dismayed to realize that he has forgotten nothing: all the dishes are on the table along with their dressings and serving utensils. There is ice water; there are condiments; there are even toothpicks in a pewter dispenser. He has no more excuses to jump up and run to the kitchen.

Joseph picks at his dinner. His throat feels narrower than usual; the food, even the soup, does not seem to want to slide down it. Gidi and Batya have placed their aluminum-wrapped meals on his dishes, but the others are eating his meal heartily, putting a bigger dent into the platters of beef and chicken and the deep bowls of salad than he guessed they would. The potato *roesti* is particularly popular.

In fact, the only thing that passes Joseph's lips without trouble is the merlot, which he has been steadily consuming. He is pleased to note that Noam, Ethan, and Gavri have been keeping pace with him, and that Batya and Gidi, too, have emptied a fair portion of their own bottle of sweet red; only Daniel stopped after the first glass. Joseph takes three swift gulps from his wineglass and clears his throat.

"Do you boys still like to sing Sabbath songs? I thought maybe you would . . ." He jumps to his feet too quickly and steadies himself on the stone table. He weaves toward the buffet table under the hunting scene, removing a cellophane-wrapped packet of song booklets that he begins to distribute among his guests. "Please," he says as he passes them around the table, "please choose a song."

The boys and Batya thumb through their booklets. They do not meet one another's glances. Joseph resumes his place at the foot of the table and thumbs through his booklet, too. "*'Yah Ribon,'* perhaps, or how about *'Tzur Misheloh'*?" He is practically begging.

Gavri is the first to sing, an under-the-breath wordless hum that blossoms into the first verse. Tears of gratitude pool in Joseph's eyes, but he waits to join the singing until the others have. They sing the old, slow tune with feeling, so that even Batya forgets herself and adds her voice. The candles jump and flicker. Someone sings harmony and Joseph leans back in his chair, letting an incautious thought slip into his mind: that perhaps this reunion will pass without incident, that he and his sons will have come together in peace after twenty years.

The boys have stopped eating. Only Batya is still picking at her food. More than once Joseph has caught her eyeing the forbidden dishes that have been passing in front of her. Gidi noticed, too, and moved a plate of chicken breasts out of her reach. "How about singing *'Dror Yikrah'* while I clear the table?" Joseph does not wait for them to begin singing before he takes two serving dishes and heads for the kitchen.

Batya immediately begins moving the scraps from one plate to another, but Ethan stops her. "No stacking dishes in *this* house," he whispers congenially. "Our father would rather make a dozen trips to the kitchen than breach etiquette."

The boys continue singing until Joseph has removed the last of the dirty dishes and plates of food from the enormous table. Before returning to his seat he opens a drawer in the buffet and takes out a small packet of cards tied up with a silver ribbon, which he places facedown next to his napkin. "And now," he announces ceremoniously, "it's time for a little entertainment.

"First, I'd like to offer a very short *d'var Torah* to you all, something I read the other day that resonated perfectly for me. On this Sabbath, we are instructed to remember what the Amalekites did to the Jewish people as we departed from Egyptian slavery. We are told to 'blot out the remnant of Amalek' wherever we find it, in every generation. Well, in a lovely little book of biblical exegesis called *From the Mouth of God* we learn that blotting out the Amalekites does not mean we should seek to annihilate a human being, since we have no way of really knowing who the descendants of Amalek are today. Rather, we are expected to blot out our own misgivings and doubts, which the author claims are the real enemy. We can do this, he says, through the same formula for expiation that we use on the Day of Atonement, namely prayer, repentance, and charity, which we learn from the expression 'to blot out' as it is used in several places in the Talmud. Now, with the author's permission, I would like to add a fourth variant to the formula: forgiveness. It often seems to me that the other three rely on our ability to forgive others' transgressions, as well as our own. So on this special Sabbath may we all begin the process of forgiveness that will enable us to reach our highest potential." Joseph smiles and turns his palms upward in a gesture of supplication.

Gavri asks, "Who wrote *From the Mouth of God?*"

Before Joseph can speak, Daniel answers. "Rabbi Yoel Rosenzweig, of very blessed memory."

Joseph and Daniel stare at one another across the table, the one stunned and the other defiant. Joseph has never so much as uttered Yoel's name in his sons' presence, and this intimacy of Daniel's with the rabbi's work unsettles and unnerves him.

"Gideon prepared a *d'var Torah*, too!" Batya says excitedly. Gideon scowls at her but reaches into his breast pocket for his notes nonetheless. Obviously eager for the opportunity, he ignores the tension at the table and plunges into a recapitulation of a sermon delivered by his father-in-law, his rebbe, one year earlier on this same Sabbath of Remembrance. His brothers quickly lose interest as he slips back and forth between Hebrew and Yiddish, a language they do not understand. His stories are episodic and rambling.

Finally, Noam can take no more. "Why do your stories always take place in Eastern Europe two hundred years ago? Shit, Gidi, why would any of this be relevant to us in late twentieth-century Israel?" His cheeks are red and he is sitting up very straight in his chair. He throws an apologetic look to Batya, who is mortified.

Gideon answers quietly, as if to a child who needs calming. "Some of our greatest rabbis since the times of the Talmud lived in Poland and Russia in the past few centuries. As far as Yiddishkeit is concerned, modern Israel is a wasteland. It's where Jews are Jewish in name only, worse even than all the assimilated people in America. Pork eaters. Sabbath desecraters." Gideon turns his attention from Noam to his father. "Sodomites." He smiles and continues. "In fact, the biblical commentator Rashi argued that the Amalekites polluted the Israelites by pederasty. They debased themselves and the Israelite men by lying with them. For this sin we are reminded to blot them from the earth, to remove them from human and divine memory. This is truly the sin of all sins."

"Oh fuck this, I've had enough," says Noam, pushing his chair away from the table.

"No wait, please," Joseph begs.

Gideon continues. "There is not a single modern Israeli rabbi whose brilliance reaches even the ankles of someone like the Gaon of Vilna or any of his disciples."

"Rabbi Yoel Rosenzweig, of very blessed memory." All eyes turn to Daniel, but Daniel's gaze is riveted on his father.

"Father, do you hear Gideon?" Noam fumes. "Are you listening to what he's saying? He's insulting us, each and every one of us. He's holier than us all and has come to tell us what's wrong with us. Well, I for one don't need to hear this from anyone, my sainted fucking brother included."

Joseph picks up the packet of cards from the table and waves them desperately at his guests. "I've made a small game," he says quickly, afraid of losing them, "a trivia game of sorts, about our family. I thought it would be fun to revisit some of our happy memories and share family lore with our newest member." He gestures grandly to Batya, who gazes down at her lap, blushing. The boys are silent. Several shift in their chairs. Noam groans and buries his face in his arms but does not leave the table.

Joseph continues, frantic to improve the atmosphere. "It'll be fun. You'll see. Here we go, first card. Who were the Raskin family?"

Noam moans into his arms, Daniel is silent. Gavri and Ethan share a discreet glance, then Ethan decides to rescue his father. "Our neighbors in Cambridge. They had a girl my age who probably still hates boys thanks to us. She was an only child, and we were a pack of wild boys. One of us would always fall on her or smash into her and send her flying. She was traumatized."

"Right!" Joseph nearly shouts. He tosses the card to Ethan, who waves it in the air like a winner. "Now who can tell me," Joseph says, brandishing a second card, "what color our tractor was?"

Gavri laughs. "Too easy, Dad. It's still parked behind Grandfather's cottage."

Daniel adds, "You left, but it never did."

After an uneasy silence, Joseph tries again. "In 1973, three events of great importance to our family—"

"Enough!" shouts Daniel. "This is pathetic. It isn't going to work, so quit trying."

Joseph puts the cards back onto the table and guzzles the remaining wine in his cup. He takes a deep breath, leans back, and surveys his small audience, who, around the enormous table, seem to be a great distance away. He takes them all in without moving his head.

"Daniel's right. My apologies to you all for trying too hard. You simply can't know how much it means to me to have all five of you boys, and now even my lovely new daughter-in-law, together for the first time after so many years. There is no better gift for my fiftieth birthday." What he does not say is: Does anyone feel bad about not bringing even the tiniest present? Some silly tie or pair of slippers, or the latest corkscrew? Tel Aviv has recently joined the ranks of cities with shops for men, shelves full of expensive, useless junk for the man with everything. Did you never think to bring me something, alone or together, a token, a card, a certificate? I send you boys handmade sweaters and tickets to shows and meaty checks for birthdays. I make occasional disbursements, when an investment pays off or a bond comes due, of sums large enough to travel abroad or buy a motorcycle. I put money discreetly into your savings accounts and maintain pension plans for you all. I worry about you, anticipate your needs, tend to your future so you can enjoy your present. When will you stop punishing me?

It is Pepe who has inspired this unspoken tirade. Their coldness, their collective, insatiable sense of being owed something has always infuriated Pepe, who has lectured him on this subject so many times that Joseph refuses to discuss the boys with him anymore. He is jealous of Pepe's relationship with his daughter, a young woman from whose life he has been totally absent but who seems grateful for every attention from him. And Joseph has offered so much to his sons over the years, which they repay with truncated phone conversations, snubbed birthdays, and a complete lack of graciousness at every gesture of generosity.

"Turning fifty is more momentous than I thought. I keep taking stock of my life and I feel I've been very lucky, or blessed, despite some very difficult decisions I have made along the way. But more than focusing on the past, I'm becoming obsessed with the future. And you boys, and Batya, are very much a part of that." He crosses his legs and raises his empty wineglass in a toastlike salute. "For twenty years you have been holding my choices against me, each of you in your own way. And I have paid dearly for that and worked hard to overcome it. I have swallowed many, many insults from you all and endured endless humiliations. But you have never tried to understand who I am and why my life has taken the path it has. So I have a few things to say to you tonight."

Batya nervously bites a nail. The twins look down into their laps. Ethan, pained, stares at the middle of the table and Noam surveys his brothers' faces, a mischievous smile on his own, pleased to see some real action. Daniel alone looks at Joseph over the cluttered table. Joseph senses his displeased anticipation in his narrowed gaze and pursed lips. He speaks to them all but looks at Daniel.

"You can't know what my own little hell was like for all those years. I was bumping around inside myself, desperately unhappy and not even knowing what it was I wanted, what exactly was wrong. Every night I tried to count my blessings, the beautiful healthy children, the successful career, the loving wife, and every night I came up short. 'So what's wrong?' I would ask myself, and I never had an answer. When I think back on those days, our years in Cambridge, and then back on the moshav, or before then, as an only child with a sad and lonely mother and impossible father, I wonder how I functioned as well as I did. Army, marriage, fatherhood, a doctorate. Teaching, writing, publishing. There were so many demands and I seemed to be managing them all.

"But I wasn't, really. I was so short-tempered with you all. By the end your mother could barely manage to do anything right in my eyes. I was all criticism and no appreciation. The five of you were a handful, so close in age, so much energy, but I retreated to the university, where I could succeed at what I was doing, and your mother was left on her own to handle you and the house and my father and the animals." He considers stopping here. Maybe he has made his point, or enough of it anyway. But no, this has been more of an apology than an attempt to explain himself, so he pushes on.

"It was then that I met someone who would change my life, a rabbi, an *illui* the likes of whom none of you will ever, ever meet. Ask any religious person who Rabbi Yoel Rosenzweig was, and they'll tell you—the greatest, the wisest of his generation." Several of the boys look at Daniel for a reaction, but none is offered. "Everyone remembers something different about him, and it was all true. He could quote whole tractates from the Babylonian Talmud, had memorized the Jerusalem Talmud, too, for comparison. He could recite a thousand poems from medieval Jewish Spain alone, spoke a half dozen languages, and read a dozen more. His scope included everything. He swallowed complex tomes of physics, biology, chemistry; studied anthropology, archaeology, sociology; knew both Jewish and general history as though he'd lived in every age in every country. But he loved literature and poetry the best. He was the great synthesizer, a giant of a man more powerful than a bear and gentler than a kitten. His lectures were attended by thousands. No hall in Jerusalem could contain the overflow and eventually he was put on television to accommodate the crowds.

"He was also a very conflicted man. I noticed it the first time we met, when I approached him for help with my first book. It wasn't just his enormous proportions, the huge body with the brain of a computer. It was his sad eyes, the look of a man who could not appreciate his many gifts because he was overwhelmed by the burden, the responsibility. He saw this conflict in me, too, and that's how we became . . . friends."

Joseph feels energized. He leans forward in his chair and returns his glass to the table. They are listening, this tiny, important audience of his. Daniel's gaze may have softened, Noam has not fled the table, and the other three boys are looking not at their plates, not at the paintings on the walls, but at their father. His success is palpable. He is winning them over slowly, and he has not yet penetrated to the core of his story. Now he selects his words with utmost care. He must make them see the unfolding of events through his own eyes. Their own personal histories have sheltered them too much to allow them to sympathize with anything sordid or shameful.

"Our friendship blossomed. We spent as much time as possible together and became very, very close. He had four children and we spent time comparing notes about raising you all. He helped me find sources for my book; I treated him to fruit and spices from our garden." Joseph weighs the rapt attention of his listeners and dares to continue. "It's not an exaggeration to say we loved one another deeply. We took seaside walks together when I could entice him to leave Jerusalem for half a day. We picnicked in a poppy field near the caves at Guvrin. We hiked in the Carmel Forest and explored the Arab *shuk* in the Old City. But mostly we spent long, quiet hours together talking and studying."

This unburdening is wonderful; he thinks he could soar above this table and hover there. *Tell them everything*, Pepe has urged him. Joseph supposes he is doing just that, except for the most intimate details they would be loath to hear anyway. *Tell them you made love to one another. Tell them how. Tell them how you felt about it, tell them, tell them, tell them.* In their three years together Pepe has prized these stories out of Joseph's mouth, making him say words he had never uttered in his life. *Say those words to your sons. Tell them what really happened.* Joseph is deliriously thankful that Pepe is not here now. He can tell his sons what they need to know without shocking them. He is winning them over, gaining their respect and understanding at last. Soon he will earn their sympathy.

"One thing that bound us together was the unhappiness we were both experiencing in our marriages. To put it in terribly simple terms, he and his wife were too dissimilar, while your mother and I were too much alike. We were, after all, second cousins and you just can't escape your genes sometimes." Ethan chuckles. Gavri nods in agreement. "It became clear to us both that we needed to separate from our wives, that while these two women themselves were not necessarily the source of our grief and frustration, they could not help but exacerbate our feelings. We both understood that this would be difficult for our families. There were no precedents for divorce in Sde Hirsch and almost as few among Jerusalemites, especially for a rabbi of his stature. We planned to live together, for support. We knew we would get along well, help one another with family issues and careers, and save money by sharing rent and expenses. We settled on Tel Aviv, where we would be halfway between our two families and where we could both find employment.

"That last Saturday at home was hell. It was cold and rainy and you boys were cooped up in the house all weekend. I don't ever remember there being so much noise as on that Shabbat. One of the twins—Gidi, I think it was—was running a fever, and Daniel, you were going through a privacy phase where you'd clobber Ethan and Noam for coming into the room you all shared when you didn't want them to. Your mother had tried to finish stripping the paint off a piece of furniture on Friday and didn't get to all the cooking she'd planned. By Saturday lunch we were short on food and you boys, who usually picked at and complained about every-thing, suddenly developed tremendous appetites, all five of you. Grandfather, of course, could not be expected to do without, so your mother and I gave away our portions and nibbled biscuits that afternoon. It was then, over biscuits and tea in the kitchen, with the five of you hooting and hollering nearby, that I told her I was leaving."

You see, Pepe, they don't ask questions. They don't want to know what I am not telling them. They want my version. Maybe later, at home in their beds in another week or anoth-er month, perhaps then they will ask themselves questions, wonder about events and emotions I did not discuss. But they will not pick up the phone to ask. They will not consult their brothers. Gidi will not lean into his wife to share his thoughts or a question. I know these boys.

"You were all sent to bed early that Saturday night. I bathed the little ones and wondered when I would have that pleasure again. Your mother was stone silent, but she func-tioned. I don't know how either of us managed, especially her. We were in some sort of trance, I suppose, just doing what we always did. Ethan was the last to fall asleep. I think he sensed something. You plodded into our bedroom in those furry slippers—do you remember that pair Tante Lotte gave you? You had names for them even."

"Bunny and Runny," Ethan says hoarsely, without a smile.

"Bunny and Runny," repeats Joseph, nodding. "You came into the room and before I had even started packing, before I'd taken out a suitcase, you asked where I was going. I didn't know what to answer. I barely knew myself and had no idea why you were asking that question. But I was wearing a beret instead of a *kipa*, which gave me away to you. And you wouldn't go to sleep until I agreed to lie next to you and sing you a goodnight song.

"I packed quickly, left a note for your mother that I'd prepared on Friday, said goodbye to her in the kitchen, kissed you each in your beds, and left. I think I cried all the way to Tel Aviv.

"That night I found a place to live, just stumbled into the first apartment I saw with a FOR RENT sign posted out front. The next morning when I woke up I was so totally confused. On the one hand I loved the sunlight flooding the small, barely furnished apartment, the quiet, the sense of having a choice—when to get up, what to eat, what to do that day and for the rest of my life. On the other hand I was desperate for your morning noises, the way you'd burrow your way under our covers and race to be the first to wake us up. You big boys would try everything to make yourselves wake up before the twins and Ethan usually won, but Gidi and Gavri were little speedies, always up with the roosters. Noam was the only one who ever needed to be wakened. He'd usually stagger in when all the rest of you were already fussing and fidgeting under our covers, and we'd all laugh at his messy curls and sleepy eyes."

They laugh lightly, remembering. Noam shakes out his mane, the curls so much longer than back then, twenty years ago. "His pajama bottoms were always twisted around sideways, or he'd be wearing only one slipper!" says Gavri, chuckling.

"It was the most frightening moment of my life," Joseph continues, slightly irritated by the mirth this memory has provoked. "I had built this life with your mother and brought five wonderful boys into the world, and I was terrified at what I was in the process of doing.

"It took forever in those days to get a phone line—months and even years, in fact. Pay phones weren't that plentiful and often they didn't work. It was after noon before I managed to phone Jerusalem to tell Yoel I had left home. But I couldn't reach him. All day I went back and forth between my new flat and the pay phone, calling his office, occasionally calling his home. This continued through Monday, and by Tuesday morning I'd made up my mind to set out for Jerusalem to find him. I was making breakfast when I heard the news on my transistor radio: *The young Torah genius Rabbi Yoel Rosenzweig was found dead in an apartment in the Old City.*" Joseph pictures that apartment, often their secret hideaway for lovemaking, but keeps that memory to himself.

"I wanted to attend the funeral, to see for myself that this could really have happened. But I could hardly move myself from that little apartment I had hoped to share with him. Even in Tel Aviv there were terrible rumors about his death. The streets were abuzz with the news of it. A suicide, they said. 'Then why was he allowed to be buried on the Mount of Olives, with the holiest of the holies, the first to be redeemed when, God willing, the Messiah liberates us all from this world?' 'He lost his mind; the chief rabbi said so. How can you blame him for his actions?' I'll tell you all, he had more of a mind than anyone in this world. It wasn't something he could lose.

"I have tried for years to understand, to accept what happened, my fate and his. I have recovered from those days only thanks to time, but sometimes, when I'm feeling most alone, those wounds seem as fresh and raw as if they'd happened yesterday, and the love I felt for him seems not to have dissipated over the years, but to have grown and flowered. He would have been in his mid-fifties by now, probably a bald old grandfather. We might not have gotten along after all. We might each have remarried or simply followed different paths. But there are three things for which I can never, ever forgive him: for opting out of this world when he could have made a world with me, and for failing to share his feelings with me, his misery, when I, more than anyone, could have helped him find his way."

There is a short silence until Ethan asks in a gentle, coaxing voice, "What was the third reason, Father?"

As Joseph looks around the table it seems to have shrunk, pulling his sons and Batya unbearably close to him. "I once gave him a marvelous gift, the most wonderful thing I have ever owned, an ancient glass bottle that Arik Shushinsky found at the beach and passed on to me."

"Arik from the moshav? Assaf's father?" Ethan finds it hard to believe Joseph could have received such a gift from his best friend's father. He has never known Arik to give a gift to anyone, let alone to Joseph, a man he openly loathes.

"Yes, the one and only Arik. We were the best of friends once, as kids. I got him through school for years. He owed me. Anyway, Yoel prized that bottle. No one had ever given him anything so precious before." Joseph closes his eyes and breathes deeply. He has never told this to anyone before, never let even Pepe wrestle this last secret from him. "The newspapers reported that he'd used shards of glass from an ancient bottle to slash his wrists. I understood right away: he'd made me the instrument of his death."

When Joseph opens his eyes, the room seems transformed. The light is dimmer; the shine and sheen have evaporated and there are puddles under the goblets and decanters. Joseph is not yet certain whether this unburdening will bring him the release he longs for. His boys seem moved, however.

Ethan is the first to break the silence. "I think I speak for us all when I say we had no idea. I mean, it must have been awful for you. . . ."

Gavri adds in an awestruck voice, "It's like you're a Righteous One, punished on the spot for your transgressions."

Gidi nods and Batya smiles.

"Why didn't you tell us any of this before?" asks Noam. "Why did you keep this all to yourself?"

"Well, I was never sure you were really ready to hear it all. In fact, I wasn't sure now either, but turning fifty makes me realize I have to put things in order, and first on my list is my relationship with you, the people I love most in the world."

Daniel has been silent throughout his father's story, quiet and enigmatic as they all expect him to be. Now, as if awakening from a long, deep sleep, he shouts across the table at his father, startling everyone. "But you love yourself more than you love any of us, more than you loved Rabbi Rosenzweig, and certainly more than the old Brazilian fart who keeps you here like a whore!"

Joseph does not move a muscle, does not blink, does not make a sound.

Daniel speaks quietly now, with malice, and suddenly Joseph feels the true menace. "That was a lovely story, Father, really. If it were anyone else telling it I would probably have bought it and fallen for the poor, misunderstood soul. But all of us sitting here, we're the victims of your selfishness and recklessness, so now I'm going to tell you a story, too."

Joseph has never seen such a look of sheer hatred, especially on Daniel. Moody and brooding, yes, but never ruthless. He understands that his eldest son is about to pay him back for all his sins, whatever Daniel perceives to be his crimes. He is about to receive the cruelest punishment of his life. How ironic, thinks Joseph, as he realizes this is the release he has been searching for all along. He cannot wait for Daniel to continue.

Daniel has shifted to the edge of his chair. "Do you have any idea what it was like to be your son? I remember your rages, the hysteria about finishing your doctorate in Cambridge. You made life miserable for Mother, for all of us. I think I peed in my bed every night that year. It got to the point where I took to sleeping bottomless on a sheet of plastic covered with a towel to save Mother the bother of washing pajamas and sheets and blankets on a daily basis. You were out of the house from dawn until late at night, but that was better than when you were around, like on Shabbat. In shul everyone thought you were more lenient than the other fathers because you let us play outside during services. But I knew it was because you didn't want us around. You were afraid we'd make noise and bother or embarrass you. Noam, Ethan, do you remember the game we used to play? *Don't wake the giant?* I would pretend to be asleep and you two would make noise and taunt me and then I'd scream and holler and beat the shit out of you both."

Ethan nods solemnly. Noam has a quizzical look on his face; he does not remember.

"Those months when we were alone in Israel, while you finished your work in America, were the best in my life. I loved speaking Hebrew again, made lots of new friends, and thought nothing could be better than helping Grandfather pick fruit or feed the chickens. Best of all, you weren't around. But then you came back and things were worse than ever."

Joseph cannot help wondering how much of this Daniel really felt during those years and how much is anger that he has projected onto the past. Is Joseph Daniel's great excuse for not succeeding in life? Joseph remembers him as dreamy and distracted, more withdrawn and contemplative than most kids his age, rarely a smile on his face. Each of his sons provoked a different reaction from him when he looked in on them in their beds. The twins were roly-poly red-cheeked tykes who made him laugh. Noam was pure mischief; he exuded impish confidence even in his sleep, and while his pranks and wiles caused Joseph no end of grief, they also tagged him as a child who would always manage to take care of himself, so Noam commanded his respect. Ethan's attitude was no-nonsense, and even asleep he demanded to be taken seriously. But with Daniel, Joseph's emotion always bordered on pity. Such a beautiful, clever boy, never quite happy. It was impossible to fathom where his head was, what was bothering him, what he really wanted. Joseph felt quite sure Daniel himself hadn't a clue.

"Are you listening, Father? I want you to hear every word of this." Daniel's cheeks are flushed. Joseph gives him his full attention.

"When you left we didn't see you for weeks and weeks. Mother told us you were busy in Tel Aviv. Then she said you had to go to America for a short trip. That first week she kept burning herself, scalding herself with boiling water or touching the coils in the oven. We used to think she had hands of steel; she could touch the hottest pots without flinching, but that week she managed to sear her fingers countless times. Everything seemed wrong. Then, a few days later, Bina Hartog asked if it was true that my father had left home because my mother was having a relationship with Grandfather. I didn't even understand what her words meant, but I beat her up anyway and went home to ask Mother about it. She smelled vile, Mother did. I don't think she'd showered or brushed her teeth all week. I wasn't so upset when she didn't answer me. I just wanted to escape, to run to a different room or out of the house.

"That night I thought I heard a crash in the bathroom. I lay in bed for a few minutes before getting up to investigate. I was afraid terrorists had broken in to kill us all, and since there was no longer a father in our house I would have to fight them off alone. Very quietly I put on my Shabbat shoes, my heaviest pair, in case I would have to kick any of the terrorists to prevent them from bolting before the police could catch them. As I was tying the laces Ethan sat straight up in bed and asked if I'd heard a crash, and the next thing we knew one of the twins was screaming in his bed down the hall.

"I sent Ethan to take care of Gidi. Lucky for us, Noam and Gavri slept through the whole thing. I went toward the crashing sound, expecting to find six or seven Arabs in *keffiyahs* crouching behind the old bathtub. Instead I found Mother out cold on the bathroom floor. There was an empty bottle of pills on the counter and a smashed bottle of whiskey or vodka near her head. There was a little bit of blood but mostly a terrible stench of alcohol that made my eyes water. Mommy's face was in a puddle and when I rolled her over I got a sliver of glass in my thumb.

"Ethan came down the hall carrying Gidi just as I was

trying to figure out what to do. Gidi was red and feverish, and he had snot smeared across his face from all that crying. Ethan screamed and then Gidi screamed and I sent them both to the porch to calm down. I knew I had to think quickly, that Mommy might die or that maybe she was already dead. I was too afraid to run to Grandfather's house because no one ever dared disturb Grandfather's sleep, so I made a decision to bring Mommy back to life myself. I sat her up straight by heaving her up from behind, and I propped her against the bathtub. Then I started shouting into her face and pulling her hair and pummeling her cheeks with my fists. I tried scratching her and pinching her arms with tiny, painful pinches, the kind I gave Ethan and Noam when they really got to me. Just as I was about to give up and tell the other boys she was dead, she opened her eyes wide, puked sludge all over me and herself, and came to her senses. She got to her feet slowly, threw us both into the shower in our pajamas, and stood there hugging me under the hot water until the puke and the stench were all washed away. We found Ethan and Gidi much later, huddled together and sound asleep in a corner of the porch, and when Mommy moved them to their beds Ethan woke up and asked her if she had died and come back. 'Yes,' she answered, 'but I'm back forever now.' I didn't trust her, though, and I kept watch over her for a month until the night she came to tuck me in and whispered in my ear, 'Thank you for saving my life,' and I knew she was OK."

They are all mesmerized by Daniel's story. Each one seems to be trying it on, wondering where he was and how much he knew. Ethan asks clarifying questions, like "Did you find Gidi and me under the red stepladder?" and "Was Mommy wearing a coarse blue nightgown with a small tear at the knee?" Joseph cannot imagine Rebecca trying to end her life, what with five little boys right there in the house, in her charge. And yet, she could be absolutely bullheaded at times. Daniel's story is so real that he finds himself thinking about the speckled floor tiles in that old bathroom for the first time in twenty years. They could have missed the crash and found her dead on the floor in the morning. What would he have done then?

"We bore the brunt of your decision, Father. We are still bearing it. This is your legacy to us. I will never trust a soul again. Ethan's confidence is nonexistent. Noam is loved by everyone but loves no one. Why do you think Gidi and Gavri are so religious? You again. Ideology, politics, religion, anything but your brand of rampant hedonism. How did Gidi come to marry Batya?" He switches to English: "Damaged goods. She was raped as a girl and has never been the same since. Gidi is considered damaged goods, too, in the ultra-Orthodox world, with a father like you."

Joseph looks to Gidi, who avoids his gaze. Batya stares silently at her plate. One enormous tear rolls its way slowly down her pale cheek.

Just then the phone rings. Joseph half expects it to be Rebecca calling to contribute her side of the story. But this is the Sabbath, and she would never use the phone on a Friday night. The answering machine picks up the call in the next room, and they all hear the message: *Bon soir et Shabbat Shalom, cheri, c'est Philippe. You are a beast for not calling to thank me for saving your meal. Was it délicieux? I'm sorry you didn't invite me to meet your beautiful boys. Dommage. The big news is that my sex-starved North African has asked me to move in, so if you need my services you must call me there. I'll ring*

*tomorrow to give you the number. Amitiés à Monsieur Pepe.
Ciao!*

There is no use explaining Philippe. Joseph figures the
truth really is not far from what they all must be thinking,
and what does it matter after Daniel's story anyway?

Daniel is on his feet, on his way out of the dining room.
He stops near his father's chair. Joseph is prepared for a blow
to the head, choking hands at his throat, anything. He will
not resist.

"Why didn't you tell us the truth—that you fucked his
balls and his brains out, that you twisted the mind of the
greatest rabbi of your generation? Rabbi Rosenzweig would
never have met that fate if it hadn't been for you. Didn't he
tell you so by killing himself with broken glass from the bottle *you* gave him?"

Daniel leaves the room. Noam stands, stretches, and says
in an offhand manner as he departs, "You're all crazy and
I've had it with this family." All the others whisper the grace
after meals and file out of the dining room without a word.
Joseph is left alone at the table.

The Shabbat timer suddenly shuts off almost all the lights
in the apartment. Joseph does not move from his chair in the
darkened dining room. He hears doors opening and shutting
but he cannot tell who has left the apartment and who has
stayed, if anyone. He realizes they never ate the blueberries
or cut the Birthday Cake. Maybe things would have turned
out differently if they'd just seen those blueberries?

He watches as the room comes back into focus. Is this the
same room he worked so hard to make shine? The floor, the
supple wood, as black now as the sky, as the beach below.
Wilted flowers, tarnished silver, spotted crystal, stained

linens. Isn't it always like this; everything becomes refuse, ruin? He tries to remember which prophet said, "Many shepherds have ravaged my vineyards and made my pleasant field a desolate wilderness; the whole land is waste and no one cares."

Joseph wonders if he himself even cares. He would like to cry out at the pain he has brought his boys, now men, but he feels numb. Maybe, he reasons, this is his true punishment: the will to react but the inability to feel.

Suddenly his beloved Yoel is there with him in his dark and messy vacated dining room high above Tel Aviv. For the first time since his death, Joseph truly sees him as he was. His beard and mustache are full, and the hues, in this darkened room, more dazzling than ever, the color of cinnamon sticks dripping with honey, illuminated by some distant, mysterious sun. His gray-green eyes are the shade of the winter sea and his once-pale skin seems ruddier, healthy and robust. He stands as tall and broad as he did twenty years earlier. His wide-spread legs suggest a sexuality he was once loath to own, and Joseph finds himself aroused by this—apparition. It is Yoel at thirty-five, and for a moment Joseph does not feel fifty. Pepe and Philippe do not exist and his sons are still children.

The relationship that he and Yoel shared was neither cheap nor manipulative, but he realizes Daniel and the others will never be able to comprehend completely his version of events. And maybe, he ponders, his version is wrong, too. To Joseph it is suddenly clear that every actor in his life has a different interpretation of that relationship, each to suit his own needs: for Daniel it is the unspeakable sin against him, his brothers, and their God, a perversion, a lusting, a destructive force. For Pepe it is a titillating string of tales, full of youth and vigor, hot sex and adventure. For Rebecca, it is her immature husband's escape from reality and responsibility. But for Joseph and this apparition it was true love, a space wide enough to contain two souls and two souls only, bound at every point of their beings. That feeling Joseph is beginning to recall, that deep, heavy, pining desire to merge with him, to invade him, to explore him from the inside, see through his eyes, taste through his tongue. And to be invaded right back again.

The memory of their lovemaking floods him now as he watches Yoel in front of him, not fading, not moving. Once they began it was a constant torment until they could be together again. They were both embarrassed by their urges, by the physical need they had for one another, two bright men reduced to animal coupling. They were all over each other whenever and wherever they could be: in the sand just above water's edge, in a field of wildflowers, in a cave, under a waterfall. In a bathtub, on the kitchen floor, in a pantry, on a roof. They could barely stand to be among people most of the time, the need to touch was so strong. 'Did I really drive you mad, dear Yoel? Did I really bring you to insanity?' The apparition provides no answer in his unblinking stare. 'Did I kill you?'

The illuminating light dims and Yoel fades. Joseph does not try to stop him. He knows Yoel belongs to another world. A small figure appears at the door. It is Batya, in bathrobe and slippers. He is surprised that she and Gidi are still in the house, certain they had chosen to make the long walk to friends in Bnei Brak rather than sleep under his roof.

"Come here, dear girl," he says in a high whisper. "Come sit beside me."

Batya does as she is told. She carries such a look of innocence that Joseph has the urge to take her face into his hands and cradle it. He hopes Gidi is wise and strong enough to protect her from life's cruelties.

"I'm not used to being in such a big bedroom all alone," she says softly.

"You can sit here with me as long as you like," says Joseph, happy she has chosen him for company.

Batya smiles. She folds and unfolds a tissue. "It was a lovely meal you made. I could never make such food. I know how to make soup and chicken and potatoes but I can't make them all come out together."

"Does Gideon help you?" Joseph inquires.

"Oh yes, oh yes, he gives me encouragement. But my mother makes most of our meals. She's such a good cook, like you but not so fancy. And she can make it all be ready at the same time."

They are silent for a few minutes. Joseph would like to ask many questions, but he is drained of feeling, too tired to hear the answers.

"I think you really loved that rabbi," Batya says into the dark.

"What?"

"You loved him, didn't you? You loved him from the bottom of your heart and in your whole being. I know. That's how I love Gideon."

"Yes, I did. I still do."

"Aren't we lucky?" she says in a bright singsong. "Aren't we so very lucky?"

Joseph looks at Batya's young face, a pale moon, the room's only light.

"Very," answers Joseph with a sigh that borders on contented.

It is well past midnight when Joseph puts on an old pair of plain flannel pajamas, his favorites until Pepe complained about the inconvenience of the buttons. He is slow and relaxed about his nightly routine, but thorough, working his way from bottom to top as usual: first he soaks his feet in a ceramic basin, carefully drying the spaces between his toes and applying creams. Then he rubs lotion into his knees and elbows. Next he flosses his teeth then brushes them in the circular rotating manner his dentist insists on, a ceremony Joseph performs with near-religious fervor in hopes of being buried with his own set intact. And last, he washes his face with a medicated exfoliating soap that makes his eyes sting. His foreigner's love of the English language conjures a picture of great plants and bushes sprouting forth across his face, requiring immediate exfoliation. Normally he would run to consult the dictionary. Can one really exfoliate one's skin or is this typical American advertising hyperbole? But tonight he has lost interest in words; they have failed him, assaulted him. He wishes not to talk or even think. He wishes he could quiet his mind to avoid hearing Daniel or picturing the ravaged Sabbath table or his father, Manfred, ill and demented, or Rebecca, her arms outstretched in supplication, begging him for help.

In bed he props himself up on two thick pillows and reaches for a book or a magazine on the nightstand, anything will do. His hand shakes as he lifts the latest Meir Shalev novel and opens it to the marked page, determined to escape from the events of the evening. The characters are oddly unfamiliar to him, though he is sure he was following the story just a night or two ago.

Joseph restores the bookmark to the same page and replaces the book on his nightstand. He reaches down into his pajama bottoms, touching himself lightly, but quickly loses interest. Pepe desires him with such frequency and intensity that Joseph prizes his time alone, letting his over-burdened body lie fallow and untouched for as long as Pepe stays away. This quiet withdrawal is the secret he shares with his body; he is certain that Pepe is fooled by his will-ingness and Joseph himself is surprised sometimes at his body's own complicity, tricking him into wanting to make love even when he feels nothing could arouse him. In fact, he has never refused Pepe in their three years together. Not for the first time Joseph wonders about Pepe, what he does when his urges overtake him during his many business trips and Joseph is on the other side of the globe. Pepe has an eye for smooth skin and narrow hips, and any young fool could see he is rich and safe. Once a stifled sneeze crackled down the line from Bangkok, prompting Pepe to comment on the paper-thin walls of his hotel. Another time Joseph woke him in Havana and thought he recognized Pepe's postcoital purr, a thick huskiness his voice settles into after a night of love-making. Joseph never asks, would not know how to phrase the question. Nor does he know what answer he would like to hear. He hopes Pepe is careful and Joseph is in fact relieved when he returns from overseas depleted of energy. It gives Joseph time to reacquaint himself with Pepe's paunch and the wide spaces between his teeth that give him the look of a lecherous crocodile. It allows Joseph's body to accept invasion again.

Joseph makes one last trip to the toilet, stopping to open a window—on the far side of the room this time—before burrowing himself under the heavy comforter. The wind has subsided, leaving only a trace of misty sea air in its wake. He makes up his mind to dream of the great love of his life, to reenact a scene from their four months of perfect bliss, but instead his mind flits to fleeting scenes he would prefer to forget: unpleasant, indiscreet, confusing. The Joseph of fifty does not laugh at the Joseph of twenty-five or thirty. His naiveté is no funnier now than it was a quarter-century earlier, even from under a down comforter on the bed he shares with another man. A man old enough to have a slew of grandchildren. A man who treats him like a housewife. Instead he mourns that Joseph, so unprepared for the years ahead, so unworldly. How that Harvard toilet would haunt him for years, until today! The beginning of something, he recognizes now, the beginning of a piece of his life that had carried him to this very evening. He wishes to ponder this thought, and even raises his hand over his head to trace an arc of those twenty odd years, but the drama of the day and the lateness of the hour weigh heavily on him; his hand falls to the mattress and through the mist of encroaching sleep Joseph says goodnight to his sons and his home and his worries and wafts away, into his dreams.

Joseph awakens in his bed after a short but deep and satisfying sleep. Faint light spreads from the east but the sea remains dark and murky. His thoughts spring lightly from the boys to Rebecca to his father to Pepe, staying nowhere for long.

In the medicine cabinet Joseph finds a small box in wrapping paper he recognizes, from the boutique of a favorite goldsmith on Shenkin Street. Its gold bow winks at him under the halogen lamps. He is grateful now, ready to be pampered. He slits the ribbon and the fancy paper with a nail file but stops to register a small smile in the mirror before pulling off the top of the box.

The ring sits on a bed of pastel pink cotton wool. It is wide, wider than any ring Joseph has ever worn and for a moment it seems gaudy, ill suited to his narrow fingers, like a barrel on a skinny man. Without touching the ring he lifts the box to eye level and sees that it is really two rings, a heavy inner band with raised edges and a thin outer one that surrounds the other. The outer band is engraved with letters he knows belong to some ancient Semitic language, but this puzzle will require some work and Joseph is thankful for the diversion.

The ring is a perfect fit and not too wide on his finger after all, reaching only halfway up to the knuckle. He spins the outer band round and round, holds it close to the light, then thrusts his finger toward the mirror. It catches every reflection, shines gold light back at him from every angle. He is charmed by the ring's simplicity and glad that this year Pepe has chosen a quiet, elegant gift rather than flash and sparkle.

He fetches a pair of glasses from the bedroom then sits on the edge of the bathtub for a better look. As the tiny letters come into focus he realizes the script is ancient Hebrew, closer to Sumerian than modern Hebrew but Hebrew nonetheless. He is disappointed to decipher its meaning so quickly; by the second word he recognizes the verse from the Song of Songs: *I am my Beloved's and He is mine.* Has he ever told Pepe about chanting the Song of Songs with Yoel, or that Yoel had once etched those very words in the sand on the beach at Tantura? He is almost certain he has not.

Joseph is about to slip the ring off his finger and back into the box when he pauses to think about the conversation around the table. What could possibly be taboo now? He keeps the ring on his finger and leaves the bathroom.

Silence. More silence. A huge, empty galaxy, a soundless universe. But it is very early Sabbath morning, Joseph reminds himself. Whoever is still here is sleeping. Outside, even secular Tel Aviv takes a break, only once a week, only in that sliver of time just after the last black-clad revelers fish and fumble for keys and veer off from unwanted lovers and dear friends, no longer able to stand their own stench, and just before the dog walkers and joggers reclaim the city, rubbing the pavement smooth with their rubber-soled shoes and blinding the accidental early riser with their sunburst muumuus and candy-colored spandex leotards. Between the two groups the air seems to have been sucked out of Tel Aviv like the space between trains in an underground.

At night I lie down weeping, but in the morning, joy! Will it be joy today? He thinks that a shaky contentment, a cautious relief, is the most he can hope for.

The bedroom doors are closed, which gives him hope. He identifies Noam under a thick comforter in one room and is not completely surprised to find Gidi sprawled on a sofa facing the terrace in the living room, both the glass and screen doors flung wide open. The air is cold, but he resists the urge to slide them closed and goes instead to the kitchen. He will make a pot of tea and begin the massive cleanup that awaits him.

But to his amazement the kitchen is spotless. There are stacks of clean dishes near the sinks, pots and pans left overturned to dry, perfect rows of spotless glassware and piles of silver cutlery sorted by type: salad forks, dinner forks, dessert forks, soup spoons, teaspoons, knives, then ladles and serving forks and, at the very end, one small, curved, intricately carved silver gravy spoon lying on its back, the bowl faceup to the ceiling. The counters are wiped clean, and Joseph finds the leftovers neatly wrapped in the refrigerator. Even the sinks are immaculate, not so much as a teardrop of water in either one.

Joseph understands that he is looking for some imperfection, determined to find the flaw that will give him the advantage. The perpetrator of this act could not possibly have managed a cleanup more thorough than his own would have been, organized and executed better than he himself, supreme lord of this kitchen, could have managed. But all at once he does not care; he graciously accepts the job for what it is, the birthday gift his sons had not brought. And now that he has received this clean kitchen and the ring from Pepe, he recognizes his birth date, realizes that today is, in fact, fifty years to the day since his birth.

"Not a bad job, right?" Joseph spins on his heel to find Gavri perched on a stool at the counter by the window, framed by the gray-black sky just beginning to show streaks of colored sunlight from the east. He is still dressed in his Sabbath clothes, his white shirt loose at the bottom, *tzitzit* fringes dangling from underneath. "Batya was amazing. You can tell she's been doing the dishes for a large family her whole life. There was no stopping her! And you should've seen her ordering us around in here. Ethan learned a few things about commanding his troops, and she even managed to get Noam—Noam!—to share a bit of the work. Truth is, we had a lot of laughs."

A rain cloud of jealousy sweeps for a moment over Joseph's heart, then moves on. "I'm glad you had fun together, and I'm amazed to find the kitchen in such great shape this morning. I thought I had hours of work ahead of me. I just can't imagine how you managed all this without making a terrible racket."

"Oh, we were noisy! We kept shushing each other, expecting you to straggle in in the middle of it."

Gavri is buoyant, radiant even. He grins and shakes his head, a small, private joke bubbling to the surface.

Joseph cannot keep from lightly tapping the skin around the bruise of their lives. "What did you all talk about for so long?" One word more and his voice would catch.

"Nothing. Everything."Gavri looks up at his father. "Do you remember the cat we had in Cambridge? Ginger colored, with stripes. It's like the only thing at all I can picture from then."

"Yes," Joseph says cautiously, trying to remember.

"It was called Ginger Thumper because the older boys couldn't agree on a single name. Noam and Ethan said it was the most neurotic animal they've ever seen, nothing like the flow of pets we had back on the moshav. Spent all its time trying to avoid contact with human beings, especially us five rambunctious boys." He laughs. "They said I was the worst, that I'd chase the poor thing around for hours, but even then the cat would never, ever leave the apartment. Ethan says Mom liked the cat because it kept the place mouse-free, but you couldn't stand it. He told us how you ripped apart the house trying to get your hands on it one time when we were going on vacation for a week and the neighbors had agreed to keep her in their apartment. He said by the end, when it seemed like we'd miss our train because of the cat, you went wild, throwing pillows, overturning chairs, flipping beds over. When you finally caught Ginger Thumper she scratched you up pretty bad and you nearly strangled her in return. Daniel got so frightened he locked himself in the pantry and then we really *did* miss our train."

Vermont. Somewhere way up north near the Canadian border, in a house offered by a colleague at Harvard. Daniel did not speak to him that whole vacation. He avoided Joseph, averted his gaze the entire week. And when they boarded the train back to Cambridge and Joseph reached for Daniel's elbow the boy recoiled in terror as if bitten by a snake. Joseph remembers it all now—that mangy cat, those neighbors, the smell of the corridor that separated them. Daniel's eyes, huge and round as he watched his father nearly strangle a cat, then throw it at a wall. Didn't Ethan mention the wall as well? He'd thrown the cat at a wall, though at the last second—at the very moment his hands were about to release it, just as he could hear the pulse in his palms shout, "Harder! Harder!" just as he could already feel the deep thud, the fat and fur and bone striking plaster, maybe breaking the cat's neck, maybe splattering its guts down the bedroom wall—at that second he had relented, slightly, imperceptibly. Only he would know that he had recognized this evil in him and would not entirely succumb to that vein of violence flowing through him thick and hot as lava. His pulsing palms had stopped their shouting and the cat had grazed the wall on a toss, hit the floor, and skidded to a halt at the bed. Dazed she was, but not injured. Joseph had scooped her up and without a word to anyone carried the cat to the neighbors.

It was a terrible violence he had in him back then, nearly murderous. It occurs to him that in all his years of living alone, and later with Pepe, he has never known that feeling again. Joseph heaves himself onto the stool next to his son. "Those years were so difficult for me. I can't tell you how awful it was living with myself back then. It wasn't the cat or you boys or even your mother, only me. I was confused, over-burdened, and just plain mad at the world."

"Dad?"

"Hmmm?"

"Can I ask you something?"

"Always."

"When did you know about yourself? I mean, when did you figure yourself out?"

"You mean my sexuality?"

Gavri nods.

"Oh, I was late. Not like people today." His mind darts to Philippe. "It wasn't something people talked about."

"But when?" Gavri's voice, a pleading whine, puts Joseph on alert.

"Well," he says, "when I look back, there were tiny little clues scattered over a long period of time, even perhaps when I was a teenager." He watches Gavri's eyebrows rise in surprise. "And there were bigger clues during the Harvard years, but I still wasn't really paying attention. I suppose I didn't work it all out until I met Rabbi Yoel, and by then I was older than you are now."

Gavri nods in understanding.

Joseph feels he wants more. "It wasn't easy figuring myself out at a stage in life when so many people were depending on me. I never said it was fair. But once I had that knowledge about myself there was no turning back. Then again, I've often played the game, over the years, of imagining my life differently, you know, 'What if?' What if I'd been aware as a teenager, if I hadn't inconvenienced so many people, turned all of your lives upside down? What if I could have made the same decisions earlier, in a quieter, less dramatic way? Well, then I wouldn't have you five boys and I would be sitting here, at fifty, unable to forgive myself for ignoring the Torah's very first and most important commandment, 'Go forth and multiply.' I would have missed the richest experience life has to offer, and I would have felt I'd missed it, too."

Gavri can no longer sit still. Joseph has noticed his left foot jiggling under his chair, watched him cradle himself, but now he is exploding. He paces to midkitchen, back and forth three times, before speaking.

"What if you'd ignored it, just buried it? What if you'd prayed and repented your evil thoughts and made pacts with God to ease the burden? Couldn't you just have controlled your feelings? Couldn't you have lived from day to day, promising yourself that today, just like yesterday, you'd be good?" He is nearly frantic now, his pacing accelerated to three large steps in each direction, *tzitzit* fringes lunging forward then jerking back at each wild, syncopated turn.

Joseph leans his back against the counter and answers quietly. "No, Gavriel, I could not have lived like that." He pauses to observe his son's pacing a minute longer, deciding. "But I think we've stopped talking about me and started talking about you."

Gavri halts abruptly and the *tzitzit* fringes fall to his sides. He stares at his father, silent, and before the first sound Joseph can see the convulsions, watches his son crumple at the middle. He is quick to jump from his stool, catching Gavri on his way down and hoisting him, with difficulty, back into a standing position, embracing the full weight of his limp body.

Gavri is nearly choking on his deep sobs and copious tears. Joseph sees how new and strange crying is for him and tightens his grip while Gavri continues crying for several long minutes. Neither moves when the tears subside.

"I don't know what's happening with me." Gavri is talking into his father's shoulder. His voice is muffled and small, but Joseph thinks it has mellowed, even if only a tiny bit. "I'm so confused; it's all I think about anymore. Sometimes I think about him during prayers and I push myself into a sort of trance to concentrate, but he just keeps thrusting his way into my consciousness and it seems like I'm praying to him instead of God. I don't know if this is your fault or I was born this way, or—what does it matter? There's nothing I can do about it. I don't know anything and I can't talk to anyone, not even—not especially—my own twin brother. I *hate* this," he says with spite, and Joseph thinks he may cry again.

"One thing at a time, sweetie. Who's 'he'?"

Gavri pulls himself up and away from Joseph, then sits

on a stool, sniffing and wiping his eyes. "The head of our group of settlers. Shilo. We're best friends but I always seem to want more."

"Have you ever discussed your feelings with Shilo?"

"Are you crazy, Dad? This isn't America here. He'd never talk to me again and he'd make sure nobody else did either. And he's right. There's no place for anything like this in our lives. It's forbidden in the Torah and that's all there is to it."

Joseph sighs deeply. There are so many answers and at the same time there are none. He chooses a path. "Gavriel, you are young, and this may be nothing more than the crush every boy feels for someone he respects: his basketball coach, his camp counselor, his older cousin. Or it may be more than that." He sees Gavri wince with pain. "I can only give you one piece of advice, and it's not even mine: be true to yourself, both because you owe it to yourself and because you'll never be true to anyone else if you can't manage at least that. It's the only way a person has a chance at weathering life with any real success. Otherwise you wind up spending so much time and energy on being someone you're not that there's literally nothing left of you. That is, of course, what made me leave the family twenty years ago, but it may also be what helps you settle down into your life, marry, have a family. Just make sure you listen to yourself. That's all I ask."

They fall silent. Together they notice the sky, light now. It will be a cloudless winter day, and a bright warm sun will summon people to the streets and the parks and the beaches. Already the early walkers are out in full force.

"You won't say anything to anyone." Gavri states rather than asks this.

"I won't say anything to anyone. But I hope this won't be

the last time we have such a discussion. If anyone can understand what you're going through, it's me."

Gavri hangs his head, then lifts it as a small, wry smile curves his lips. "Yeah, that'll be fine." He places both hands on the counter and pushes himself up. "I'm gonna get myself cleaned up for morning services."

The smile of encouragement carved onto Joseph's face fades the moment Gavri is out of the room. A new worry crops up in his mind, or really just an old one suddenly made real, a worry about having somehow infected his sons. He will mull this over when the boys are gone. It will figure into the balance of success and failure of this weekend, will take its place among the events and ideas that shaped it. It will become part of the narrative, his narrative, of their family history.

The kitchen door flies open, slaps the wall, and starts to swing closed again. Gavri pushes through, pajamaed, in a headlong dash for the sink. But the change is too drastic and Joseph realizes that this is not Gavri but his twin.

"You were probably too cold in front of that open door." Gidi does not respond, his back to Joseph at the sink. Too late Joseph recalls the morning blessings—no talking until the hands have been laved and a dozen blessings recited.

After several minutes Gidi turns around. His face wears the angry scowl of a man wronged but his hair—cowlicked here, matted there—is all boy. His voice is spiked with accusation: "I had to walk more than four paces to lave and say the blessings because I forgot to put a pitcher of water and a basin next to the couch."

Joseph nearly apologizes, though he feels no remorse, and besides, Gidi's forgetfulness cannot be blamed on him.

Still, he feels sorry for Gidi, knowing this will probably ruin his day. He gestures around the kitchen. "Your wife is really something. She did one amazing job on this kitchen, better than I could have done myself. I'm sure she keeps house beautifully for you."

"For a retard she's not bad."

A hot pulse of anger shoots through Joseph's body, spitting out the unexpected response: "If that's your attitude, then you certainly don't deserve her!"

Gidi does not move from the sink. He blinks hard several times.

Joseph stares into Gidi's eyes, seeing not his son but himself, the impossible husband. Could this be yet another part of his legacy? He breathes in deeply, calming himself. "She's lovely, Gideon. A real *neshama*. And she loves you deeply. Don't ever forget or exploit that fact." He climbs down from the stool. "Now I'm going to set out some goodies for breakfast before you go to shul. You'll have a bite before you go, right?"

Gidi nods.

"Good," says Joseph, feeling he has gained a point. "Go get dressed and by the time you come back I'll have everything ready."

Gidi turns and leaves the room without argument.

Joseph knows they will eat little before shul, just enough to keep their bellies from rumbling during prayers. Still, he lays out an assortment of pastries—glazed, jellied, creamed, and frosted to perfection—and coffee, cream, sugar, hot water for tea, honey, and wedges of lemon, all meticulously and artfully arranged. He has just set the kitchen table with glass plates and cups and a fan of silver teaspoons when Gidi reenters the room, dressed and groomed now, followed by Batya.

"Good morning!" Joseph calls to Batya, his voice too loud for this early hour.

His exuberance takes her by surprise and she looks at the floor. He intuits that their midnight chat is a secret, their intimacy off-limits to Gidi. He says, softly now, "You did a brilliant job on this kitchen. It must have taken you all night."

"Oh no. Oh no. Not all night!" She is nearly breathless, her eyes and mouth round with the fear of being misunderstood. But Joseph thinks he can also detect a note of pleasure in her protest.

"Well, I never thought anyone could be more thorough than I."

Her gaze drops to the floor again.

Gavri plunges through the swinging door. "Oh good, you're still here," he says to his twin. "I thought I'd missed you. Ethan'll join us in a minute."

"Come on, everybody, have some cake and coffee before you go." Joseph shepherds them to the kitchen table. Everything is suited to Gidi's kosher standards but Joseph prefers to avoid another confrontation, so he tries a different angle. "These cinnamon pastries taste exactly like my mother's. I wasn't at all surprised to learn that the baker is Swiss, Orthodox, and about the same age as your grandmother would be today." He lifts the plate to Gidi. "Please."

Gavri and Batya look to Gidi. He stands motionless. Slowly, his eyes fixed on the pastries, he raises his fingers to the plate and takes one cinnamon roll. "*Blessed are you, o lord our God, king of the universe, who creates nourishment of every kind.*"

His small audience says, "Amen" in unison with gusto, and they all laugh. Suddenly there is a bustle, a rush to drink and eat and talk as quickly as possible. Gavri leads the final blessing and all three tumble out of the kitchen. As they prepare to leave, Joseph notices that Batya takes nothing with her and the men take only the cloth bags sheathed in clear plastic that hold their prayer shawls, so he has the final sign he needs: they will, in fact, all return to his apartment after shul; there will be a grand and happy luncheon for them all together.

Ethan emerges from the bathroom as they are standing in the doorway. "Wait up!" he calls as he ducks into the kitchen just long enough to snatch a fistful of pastries. Though all three are careful not to touch Batya, they jostle one another to the stairwell. Joseph will not ruin this moment with an offer to summon the elevator for them, and it makes him laugh to watch them play.

"It was Hillel Gross who plucked the ivory off all of Mrs. Metz's piano keys," says one son, picking up on some discussion they had had during their time washing dishes together.

"No, it was *Ariel* Gross!" calls another.

They are shouting to each other as they descend, joyously oblivious to the sleeping neighbors. Joseph lingers at the door to capture every last sound they make.

The kitchen takes no time to tidy up and lunch is still hours away, so Joseph casts about for some worthwhile way to spend his time. He considers reading a book in bed or on the terrace, thinks about a beach stroll or even a bubble bath. He feels quiet and restless at the same time. He is cautiously optimistic, imagines himself a sun with his boys in orbit around him: Gavri and Gidi, twin planets floating closer in tiny increments, just beginning, maybe, to feel his warmth; Noam and Ethan, large and self-contained, drifting at a comfortable middle distance; and in the cold outer reaches of space, Daniel, barely visible so far away. His reverie reminds him of a long-ago outing to a planetarium with the boys, and at once he knows what he wants to do.

The album Joseph is looking for is a large and bulky brown one at the bottom of the stack in the living room, but before reaching it he pauses at another, one that holds photos of their years in Cambridge. He is briefly surprised to see that he appears in only one photograph, conspicuously absent from all family outings depicted in the album. This photo, snapped by Daniel, catches him at the typewriter, a hand extended in surprised warning toward the camera. He remembers slapping Daniel for having dared touch it.

Even now, when he thinks about those years, the pressure of pursuing a doctorate at Harvard with five boisterous boys at home, he feels his face tighten, pulling around itself, taut. His mouth clamps shut and his teeth lock together. His head and neck always hurt in those years, aching to detach themselves and roll about free. At night it took him long minutes that dragged into hours to fall asleep and in the morning he awakened exhausted from dreams with too much happening in them: long lines of poetry that had to be memorized, freshly laid eggs that needed counting, the chattering of his children as they vied for his attention. All these at once. So evening tension led to morning tension, which grew throughout the day. How he envied Rebecca her peaceful slumber, her lack of urgency, and the calm, detached manner that got her through each day.

Now he relaxes his shoulders, forces his facial muscles to go slack, lays aside the album, and pulls out the heavy brown one from the bottom of the pile.

This album contains photographs of the boys collected from the years after he left home, each snapshot hard-won. Their outings never went according to his carefully planned itineraries. He had lost the family car to Rebecca, but after a few chaotic bus journeys with the boys he learned to rent an auto or hire a taxi whenever he took them out. In those days he pored over the "Fun with Children" section of the newspapers and called all the local theaters and museums in his search for appropriate cultural events. The boys made noise, fidgeted and fought; later they refused outright, Daniel in an enraged state of indignation and all the others in various levels of collusion. After a particularly disastrous outing to see a Hebrew staging of *My Fair Lady*, Joseph gave in. From then on he took them to the beach, the pool, bowling, ice-skating. On all of these excursions he would sit on hard benches watching, tying shoelaces, occasionally arbitrating fights, always providing money; later he brought newspapers with him, then novels. The photos in this album are grainy, gray, and out of focus. He had the cheapest camera available in those days, just wanting something to capture their images for a bit longer than those difficult outings.

He finds one photo that demands attention—a snapshot of Daniel, Ethan, and Noam at some sort of carnival, in front of a booth. The two younger ones seem to have formed a chaotic ring around Daniel who, placid and contemplative in the eye of the storm, stares unabashedly into the lens of the camera and through it at Joseph. He seems to be asking a question, one that begins with "Why," a question that his father will not succeed in answering.

There is a light knock at the door and Joseph half expects young Daniel will be there, with that same questioning look.

In fact, it *is* Daniel, flesh-and-blood, grown-up Daniel. He slips past his father without a word and with barely a glance, but once in the room he seems at a loss until he spots the open photo albums. Joseph closes the door and follows him to the sofa, careful to sit one cushion away from his son. Daniel leans forward to examine the photographs, and Joseph leans back to examine his son's face in profile. He wonders both where Daniel has been and why he has returned.

"Where were these taken? I don't remember any of this." Daniel flips through the album. He stops at the same photograph that caught Joseph's attention. "These must have been taken in Israel but I don't recognize anything. Is this when you were still married to Mom?"

"No," Joseph says, clearing his throat. "It was after our divorce."

"*You* took us to this fair? I don't remember ever going out with you after you left us."

Joseph lets this comment penetrate him for a moment. Could Daniel really have forgotten those outings, the time they spent together? Was he blocking out any potentially positive memory of his father? Joseph cannot resist wondering about Daniel's tale of Rebecca's near suicide. Such detail, such vivid imagery! Didn't they all sit around the dinner table last night while Daniel drew a perfect picture of that event, every sound, sight, and smell precisely registered?

Hadn't the abundance of minutiae convinced them all of its truth? But memory plays nasty tricks, never yielding every last detail. Any scene from the past should feel like an oil-painted landscape not yet finished, whole sections blank or merely sketched in pencil. Daniel's version was full, rich, and vivid. So how now can he not recall years, a whole period of his life, trips that repeated the same patterns with frightening regularity—the arguments, the awkwardness, the tension, the bitterness? These are years Joseph still frets over. It makes him laugh to think of the endless hours he spent first enduring then reliving those times, while Daniel had erased them from his memory.

"What's so funny?" For the first time Daniel looks into his father's face.

"Life is very funny sometimes. Don't you remember Rita starring in *My Fair Lady*? A picnic in Yarkon Park, when Ethan ran headfirst into a tree? The planetarium?"

Daniel pauses, poised to remember. Joseph watches him explore his mind for those events, knows he is trying to separate memory from dream and emotion and desire. He wishes he could explore with him, poking at an association here or an image there. What colors, he wonders, are this son's memories? How does he remember Joseph? Which memories are comforting and which terrifying?

Daniel's eyes flicker, then focus on Joseph. He opens his mouth to speak, looks into himself again, then stops short. "No. Nothing. I don't remember."

They sit, silent again.

"Maybe," Daniel begins after several minutes, "maybe. Did you take us once to a dig? Archaeological. Somewhere near the sea?"

Joseph nods in encouragement.

Daniel sits up straight on the edge of the couch, bright with memory. "And I found something, didn't I? A coin. I wanted to keep it. I wanted that coin in the worst way. I knew it was wrong, but I had to have it. You explained how they would clean it and catalog it, how maybe it would be put on display in a museum where lots of people could see it and I could visit it. Nothing helped. I held on to that coin like my whole life could be bought with it." He frowns, his head drooping.

Joseph continues Daniel's story. "I finally brought you to this young man, a student archaeologist, who showed you the whole process and let you hold the special brushes and sieves they were using." He does not mention the young man's perfect beauty, how Joseph had flirted with him while Daniel poked his fingers into seventh-century broken pottery. "I think he might have even let you clean it yourself. Then he offered you a trade: the coin for a beautiful piece of sea glass. The glass was worthless to them, of course, but to you—well, you were suspicious at first, thought you smelled a trick, but eventually you agreed."

Joseph is pleased with himself for remembering but notices the troubled look on Daniel's face. He knows a query, an expression of concern will not help now. He waits patiently. This much he has learned in a quarter century of trying to father Daniel.

When Daniel speaks his voice is subdued. Joseph hears in it no small amount of pain. "You know why that coin was so important to me? I remembered learning in America that your wish will come true if you throw a coin in a fountain. I figured an old and valuable coin like that would get me any wish I wanted. When I saw the coin I formed this vague plan to find a fountain somewhere. I had a pretty heavy wish to make and I needed all the help I could get."

Joseph purses his lips. He knows Daniel is waiting for him to ask about the wish, even though he knows what that wish will be. He can follow Daniel's simple plan, satisfy his son with a simple question, and give him the opportunity to unburden himself more, let him shoot yet another arrow at his father's heart. This is the price of remorse, but Joseph feels he has paid the price again and again, especially to Daniel. He knows he should acquiesce, bend to his son's needs, but something about Daniel's anger, his refusal to accept circumstances after all these years, hardens Joseph's heart.

"That suicide story you told last night about your mother," he asks instead, "did it really all happen exactly the way you described it?"

Daniel falls back into the couch with a groan. "You *always* do that. You just change the subject when you feel like it. I don't even know why I bother trying to talk to you."

"Then let's really talk, Daniel. We both know the outcome of the coin business. You wished me remarried to your mother or dead. It would have been one and the same for me." Daniel starts to protest but Joseph raises his hand to stop him. "Yes, I mean that. But it wasn't your mother who was killing me. It was the situation. It was everything expected of me that was no longer me. And in the long run it would have been the same for you and your brothers, too, having a father teetering on the rim of madness or suicide all the time." Daniel's forehead crinkles into a question but he does not interrupt. "In those days we didn't solve our problems on psychologists' couches; we didn't solve them at all. We just buried them and hoped they'd stay covered until we could join them underground ourselves.

"Yes, Daniel. You got a bad deal in fathers. A very bad deal. In fact, aside from loving you with all my heart I have been good for nothing to you. I simply could not do what was expected of me. I could not bury it all. I made a choice—the most awful, terrifying, sobering choice of my life—and I have spent the rest of my life measuring the gains and losses, inspecting the damage and patching the holes. I have been lonely and sad and sick with heart grief, but I have never, ever thought I made the wrong decision. It was simply what I had to do, what I needed to do to save myself. It was no more and no less than what a person must do if he wishes to be of any use to the people who depend on him, like those safety masks on the airplanes, the yellow ones that pop down from the ceiling in case of emergency—they always tell you to take one for yourself first, get your breath, and only then help your children. Now most of us would instinctively come to the aid of our children first and probably pass out in the attempt."

Daniel's laughter is bitter. "Well, you managed with your life mask but never gave us ours. You let Mom do it all, but one female parent for five boys just wasn't enough."

"I'm sure you're right," says Joseph, glad Daniel is finally engaged in this discussion. "But my heart in those days told me that you were all better off without me than with me as I was. That the oxygen in the masks I had to offer you was poisoned. In fact, I assumed that the greatest service I could perform for you was to drown myself in the sea. I felt guilty that I couldn't do it. Funny to recall this now, but when I lost Yoel and all of you—in the same week!—and my thoughts were incessantly, relentlessly on how to end my own life, a single verse from Psalms kept ringing in my head. It was like a chant, a monotonous incantation that I heard morning, noon, and night: *I will not die; rather, I will live to tell the word of God.* I still haven't figured it out, but as strange as it must seem to you to be hearing this from me, I always felt I had some sort of mission to fulfill, that there was some reason for me to stay alive. That perhaps one day I would be called on to testify to God's word—me, your father, the secular, sinful hedonist who willfully breaks more than one of his commandments. Ridiculous, isn't it?"

Daniel looks out at the sky and the sea, then back at his father. "No, it's not ridiculous."

"So tell me, son, what about that suicide story?"

Daniel squirms. "I don't really know," he says very softy. "I've gone over it in my mind every day for twenty years now. I reimagine it every night in bed." He adds, embarrassed, "At some point I began to believe I couldn't fall asleep without reliving the whole scene from beginning to end, from the sound of the crash to Mom mentioning it that once."

Joseph resists the urge to touch his son, to hug him or hold his hand. Daniel continues, unprompted. "The thing is, it's all so real, every bit of it, and nothing about it ever changes. And it doesn't feel at all like a dream. I barely ever remember my dreams but this is so. . . . Well, nothing about it ever fades. I feel like I could touch everyone, anything . . ." He stops, the words clogging his throat.

Joseph senses Daniel has never told this to anyone before. "Can't you simply ask your mother?"

Daniel shakes his head. "She doesn't talk about those days. We don't even talk about you to her. It would be too hard for me to bring it up. And anyway," he says, now meeting his father's gaze and holding it, "I have a feeling she's not well."

"Not well?" Joseph asks feebly, because in the same instant he knows. When he was fretting about the upcoming Sabbath with the boys she had tried to tell him something he can only now hear: *I have a problem and I will need your help.* And suddenly, just like that, he knows. That this is not only about his father, but about Rebecca as well. That they need him to walk back into their lives with the same decisiveness he used when he walked out on them twenty years earlier. That he will indeed look after them, that he will be humbled. And that something in him will heal while he tries to mend the others.

But now there is a flesh-and-blood son sitting in front of him trying to make sense of his own existence. "Daniel, my love," Joseph says slowly, pushing Rebecca and Manfred to the back of his mind until he can visit them alone, "it seems to me that I bequeathed you something far worse than a broken home and a father of questionable repute. I've kept you so busy with my legacy that you haven't had the time or the inclination to deal with yourself."

Joseph lets Daniel ruminate on this idea, then continues. "I'm not trying to excuse myself from blame. Heaven knows I carry around enough guilty feelings for all of us. But at some point you have to say to yourself, 'This is the life I was given. These are my defining circumstances. This is what I have to work with.' Certainly it will be better than what some people get and worse than others, but these are the basic facts. What you do with them is then entirely up to you. So you can spend your life angry and bitter or you can cut your losses and continue. At some point it is up to you. I only made my choices, realized what it was I wanted and how much I wanted it, when I was slightly older than you. You've just got to start to focus on you."

Daniel stands up. He pulls a small envelope, crumpled and soiled, from his breast pocket. "I left this place last night thinking I wouldn't be back, ever. I walked all over Tel Aviv and eventually wound up in my own apartment. And all of a sudden I knew I had to give this to you." He hands the envelope to his father. Joseph does not so much as glance at the return address; the crimped handwriting is enough for him. "It came the day after you left home. Twenty years ago, I can't believe it! I got it from the mailbox myself. Mom's never seen this. I took it to my room without opening it. I think I was planning to give it to you that evening when you got home; I used to pretend I was the mailman sometimes. But you didn't come home that night or any other night and the letter became a sort of prize, or a ransom I was going to lure you home with. Only I never told you about it." He shifts position, uneasy with himself. "I eventually read it after a few months, and I've kept it with me, hidden, ever since, wherever I go. In the army I treated it like a good-luck charm; it was always in my breast pocket. I've made a study of it, and it led me to read all of Rabbi Rosenzweig's books and articles. I can practically quote them. His brain was so . . . so . . ."

"Expansive," Joseph says to the hands that hold the letter he both aches and fears to read. "As deep and wide and profound as the whole universe. And as complex."

Daniel has gained his composure and is flushed with the excitement of being understood. "But I only completely grasped it last night," he says, more passionate than Joseph has ever heard him. He stops, searching the walls for the words he is missing, then finds them. "I am so very, very sorry, Father. I should have given it to you a long time ago."

This letter is much shorter than Yoel's first, the love letter. No salutation, no signature. No date.

I am sick with sin. I have discovered G-d's true purpose in bringing us together: He has tested me and I have failed. In our last meeting we unhinged ourselves from G-d and His commandments, and I have squandered the many gifts He has given me. I lack Rabbi Amram's courage and honesty to raise my voice and shout, "FIRE." I cannot cry from the housetops what I have done in the secret chamber. There is only one thing for me now: to mete out the prescribed punishment and join Him in the World to Come.

Save yourself, Joseph.

Joseph takes a deep breath, but there is not enough air in the room to satisfy him. He steps out onto the terrace. Here, high above land and sea, he can swallow all the air in the sky, gulp in a universe full of wind. At the railing, on this clear Sabbath morning in March, he shreds the letter and the envelope into tiny pieces and tosses them over the edge. They soar and swirl and disappear. Joseph turns around to find Daniel watching from the doorway. "You see, son," he shouts over the roar of wind and sea, his arms spread wide, "sometimes you just have to let go!"

Joseph walks to where Daniel stands transfixed. With only a slight pause he leans toward his son, then throws his arms around him.